"You're early," he said.

"Early?" I shook my head and made a face. "Early for what?"

The rumbling roar of cement drills mixed with the sounds of men shouting. And the clinking of metal against metal ran through it all.

"No matter," he said. "Who let you in without a hat?"

I crossed my arms over my clipboard, holding it close. "I let myself in."

He narrowed his eyes as he studied me. Then he nodded and held out a hand. "I'm Charlie Alexander, Project Engineer."

I looked at him, then shook his hand. It would just be rude to do otherwise.

"Come on," he said. "We have a meeting."

"Okay," I said, totally confused. Somehow Charlie Alexander, Project Engineer, knew who I was. I was pretty sure I had never met him.

And yet, he'd introduced himself, so he didn't think we knew each other.

I shook my head.

He was already walking toward the door that led out to the road. I followed, my heels clicking on the concrete, refusing to rush to catch up with him.

"You can ride with me," he said, stopping until I was almost caught up with him.

What the—?

"I have my own car," I said, matter-of-factly, ignoring the glance he shot in my direction.

We reached the framed-out door and walked through. I found it a little amusing that he walked through the door frame when he could just as easily have walked through one of the framed-out walls.

On the street now, he stopped and looked at me.

A late model car and an SUV passed on the road behind him. One of the concrete trucks moved, its deep motor rumbling and clattering as it pulled out of the dirt parking lot behind us.

I lifted an eyebrow and waited.

I thought I saw the shadow of a smile cross his features, but I might have been mistaken.

"We have a meeting with Noah Worthington at Skye Travels," he said, pulling his cell phone out of his inside jacket pocket.

I kept a straight face. At least I think I did. Didn't much matter. He wasn't looking at me now. He was looking down at his phone.

"Give me your number and I'll text you the address."

"I have the address," I said, not moving.

Now he was looking at me sideways. "Are you sure?"

"Skye Travels at the airport?"

"Yes." He put one hand on his hip.

I rattled off the address.

"Good enough," he said with a shrug. "Meet you there."

I watched him stride away. He definitely strode. Straight to his silver Mercedes sedan.

He got into the driver's seat, waited about two seconds, then pulled out onto the road heading to San Felipe.

I made a sound. I wasn't sure if it was a scoff or a laugh. Maybe a little of both.

Walking in the other direction, I got into my Bentley Continental GT.

Black.

Not silver. Black.

THE MAGIC OF CHRISTMAS

ALSO BY KATHRYN KALEIGH

Contemporary Romance
The Worthington Family

The Heart of Christmas
The Magic of Christmas
Second Chance Kisses
Second Chance Secrets
First Time Charm
Three Broken Rules
Second Chance Destiny
Unexpected Vows
Billionaire's Unexpected Landing
Billionaire's Accidental Girlfriend
Billionaire Fallen Angel
Begin Again
Love Again
Falling Again
Just Stay
Just Chance
Just Believe
Just Us
Just Once
Just Happened
Just Maybe
Just Pretend
Just Because

THE MAGIC OF CHRISTMAS

THE WORTHINGTONS

KATHRYN KALEIGH

THE MAGIC OF CHRISTMAS

SECOND CHANCE KISSES PREVIEW

Copyright © 2022 by Kathryn Kaleigh

All rights reserved.

Written by Kathryn Kaleigh.

Published by KST Publishing, Inc., 2022

Cover by Skyhouse24Media

www.kathrynkaleigh.com

No part of this book may be reproduced in any form or by any electronic or mechanical means, including information storage and retrieval systems, without written permission from the author, except for the use of brief quotations in a book review.

This is a work of fiction. Any names, characters, places, or incidents are products of the author's imagination and used in a fictitious manner. Any resemblance to actual people, places, of events is purely coincidental or fictionalized.

To learn more about Kathryn Kaleigh, visit

www.kathrynkaleigh.com

Kathryn Kaleigh

1

CHARLIE ALEXANDER

An orange tower crane stood sentinel over the skeleton of the mid-rise office building crawling with activity. Men scurrying here and there. Loud claps of metal against concrete. Men shouting and vehicles beeping.

Everyone had a place to be and a job to do.

The light breeze of a late-December morning in Uptown Houston carried the distinct odor of chalky concrete dust and diesel fuel.

Holding a battered wooden clipboard, a black pencil attached to the clip with a carabiner leash at my side, I stepped onto the wire caged construction elevator and pushed the up button.

The beeping of a cement truck on the ground faded seamlessly into the rumbling roar of cement drills as I traveled up to the tenth and top floor of what was soon to be the new Worthington Enterprises building.

One of the construction workers, covered in cement dust, looked up from where he knelt, hammering an anchor in concrete, nodded as I passed the third floor. I nodded back. I didn't know his name and most likely never would. But he knew me. Even if he didn't actually know my name, which was quite possible, he knew me as the one they called the big boss.

I wasn't actually the big boss. The big boss was Noah Worthington. But in their day to day world, I was their big boss. Noah had been on site a handful of times, but he had never been introduced. Slipping in and out like a shadow, he had no need to spend time on site. That was my job.

Two men shouted indiscernibly, followed by male laughter, over the sound of their power drills as I passed the seventh floor. Three other men stood by watching. The men talked more bullshit during one day than most people talked in a month.

The workers all wore yellow hardhats.

My hardhat was white.

If they didn't know by my charcoal business suit, white shirt, and gray tie that I was the engineer in charge, they would know by my white hardhat. They would at least know that I was somehow in charge. Most of them I had spoken to as group, though, some even personally.

They were used to seeing me around. Seeing me talking with their foremen. Going over designs.

A gust of wind whipped at the papers on my clipboard as I passed the eighth floor. Less than one week before Christmas and the best Houston weather could do was to drop to sixty-five degrees. As a building engineer, that was in my favor, so I took it as a win. The longer the weather held, the longer I could stay ahead of schedule.

I'd heard on the radio on the drive over here to the San Felipe site, that the weather was going to drop over the next few days, but the forecasters regrettably dashed all hopes of a white Christmas.

So different from the first eighteen years of my life when it had been odd *not* to snow on Christmas. It was a novelty here in Houston. One that I had gotten used to not expecting.

I scowled and straightened my tie. It didn't exactly affect me whether it snowed on Christmas or not.

Since Noah Worthington insisted that all work stop for one week at Christmas, all I had to do was to get this building in the dry. Basically to get the roof on.

Because of Noah's holiday declaration, even the lowest and newest man on the job got a paid one-week Christmas vacation to spend with his family.

The thing was, a lot of these men didn't have families. They would simply use the time off to take on other jobs. Noah didn't care. He insisted that every man be given the opportunity.

If some of the office staff wanted to work and were qualified, they could shift up to Skye Travels by the airport and work for overtime. Noah's private airline company required all hands on deck this time of year, so he hired extra people and rotated their time off.

As I reached the tenth floor, the elevator jerked to a stop and the door slid open with a not so comforting scrape of metal against metal.

Though the jerking and scraping was a little disconcerting, it didn't worry me. I knew the elevator was safe. I had overseen every nut and bolt of this building from the original design conception to the foundation prep to this very moment.

I walked quickly across the tenth floor to the metal stairs leading up to what would be the roof. This was that point when we had to move quickly.

We had two days to get a roof on this building before everything had to shut down for a week.

I'd never overseen a job where I had shut down construction that long for Christmas. A day maybe, at most.

I had a good crew and, with the weather on our side, we

would get it done in time for it to be in the dry before the holiday break.

Standing with the foreman on duty, I watched as the lumberous crane lowered a stack of plywood onto the tenth floor. Like King Kong gently setting a beautiful girl on top of the Empire State Building.

Twenty-five guys wearing yellow hard hats waited at the ready to begin hauling the plywood up to start framing out the roof.

I adjusted my hardhat and went to make a note on one of my check sheets. The pencil lead cracked and the broken end fell to the ground.

I checked the inside pocket of my gray suit for a pen, but all I had in my pocket was my cell phone and a white handkerchief. Seeing the handkerchief sent a familiar wave of guilt through me.

Carrying a handkerchief was a habit I had learned from my father. *Always have a handkerchief on hand in case a lady needs it.*

I smiled wryly at the old-fashionedness of carrying a handkerchief for the ladies. The ladies I knew would probably look at me like I had two heads if I handed them a handkerchief. Not that I would ever have need to do so to begin with. I had yet to come across a lady who had need of a handkerchief in the twenty or so years that I had worn my first suit at the age of ten.

But the habit was ingrained and I wasn't likely to change it. In the meantime, it wasn't helping me take down notes.

If it wasn't written, it didn't happen. Another ingrained habit.

Of course, I didn't normally have a handkerchief on the construction site, but then I didn't normally wear a suit on the construction site either.

Today was different. Today I had a meeting scheduled later with the owner of the building, Noah Worthington.

I had a distinctly sneaky feeling that as the engineer on site, I was going to be more like Noah, the big boss, who didn't get to take a Christmas break.

It was probably for the best. Because like half the men here on site, I would be alone for Christmas.

2

MAKENNA FLEMING

The Galleria was crowded this time of year.

Christmastime in Houston.

Standing on the second floor, I looked down to the ice rink below. Even the ice rink was crowded. And it was barely past nine in the morning.

The shops weren't open yet, but breakfast places were open as was the hair salon on the first floor.

The huge Christmas tree—fifty-five feet tall—took up nearly one whole end of the ice rink. Decked with thousands of ornaments and nearly half a million twinkling lights, it was topped with a large golden star.

The tree lighting ceremony was one of my favorite activities of the season, especially now that I had younger cousins to take part in the coloring contests and face painting. This year's live music had been one of the best I could remember.

The children on the ice right now were the best. They showed no fear as they performed miracles on ice. Axels. Loops. A camel spin. The ice skaters out there were advanced to say the least.

They were the ones who showed up before daybreak to get their time on the ice.

One of those seven-year-olds out there on the ice right now was my younger cousin, Sophia. Sophia was Olympic material and had performed during the tree-lighting show this year. Probably one of the main reasons why I had enjoyed it so much.

My aunt and uncle had built an indoor ice-skating rink for her and she practiced on it ALL the time. But that rink was small compared to this one. And a skater could not advance in a vacuum. So four, sometimes, seven days a week, she came to the Galleria to get time on the ice with her coach.

Since my Aunt Ainsley was a pilot, she wasn't available to cart her daughter to the ice rink seven days a week. That's where family came in.

My mother's family, the Worthingtons, were a close-knit family. We pitched in and took care of each other.

Stretching, I looked at my watch. Sophia would be ready to go by ten.

I could only sit for so long before I needed to walk around. I was currently in the middle of one of my laps around the rink. Sometimes it was hard to just walk, but breaking into a jog around the ice rink would probably not be looked up favorably.

Most mornings, not this one since it had started so early, I ran five miles around my neighborhood, weather permitting. If the weather was raining or too hot, I used my treadmill. Used the treadmill most, but it was definitely nice to get fresh air on occasion.

Sophia's session had started at six o'clock this morning and we were still here. I leaned against the railing, smiled, and waved as Sophia came out of a spin and grinned up at me.

As she skated off again, I hid a yawn behind my hand. She

had to be exhausted. I'd picked her up at her house at five a.m. and she had been on the ice since six with minimal breaks.

If I was going to get a latte, which I desperately needed just to stay awake, I needed to go get it now.

I had a lot of things to do today after I got Sophia home.

Ticking them off in my head, putting them in a logical order, I ducked off to grab a coffee. Most people made lists. I kept a paper calendar, but after a quick glance each morning, I scheduled my day in my head. Very unconventional, but I liked the mental exercise. Sort of like jogging for the brain.

I didn't have to stay at the rink with Sophia while she was with her coach, but it didn't seem right leaving her for more than a few minutes. Sophia had crashed on the ice just last year and we were all still a little bit edgy about her.

I needed to make a stop by Grandpa Noah's new building. Meet the engineer. Get him to send me some specs to review over the holidays.

As a clean energy venture capitalist, I knew a thing or two about building technology. As such Grandpa wanted me to offer any ideas I might have to make his new building more efficient.

Grandpa Worthington had built his business, Skye Travels, starting with just one airplane. Now he owned one of the largest and most successful private aviation companies in the country.

He had not stopped there. He was always on the lookout for other ventures.

Everybody said I got my entrepreneurial spirit from him and my looks from my Grandma Savannah.

I took that as the highest possible compliment anyone could give me.

Grandpa Noah was an entrepreneurial phenom and Grandma Savannah was charmingly beautiful or beautifully charming. Charming and beautiful.

The barista, a young college age boy with soulful looking eyes handed me my coffee and gave me a double-take as I smiled at him.

I considered my smile to be my secret super power and I used it generously.

As far as I could figure, a smile didn't cost a dime and the return on investment was immeasurable.

It was time to drag Sophia off the ice, get her home so she could start her day of private tutoring.

I was pretty sure that if I ever had children, I would send them to a private school, but my Aunt Ainsley wanted Sophia's education to be tailored to her own speed. So home schooling it was.

I made it back down to the skating rink just as Sophia was taking off her skates.

Seeing her happy grin made getting up at four a.m. worth it.

And reminded me that I had some Christmas shopping to do.

What did one give a seven-year-old girl who had everything, especially one who wanted nothing more than to ice skate? All the time.

If I'd been born with half of Sophia's singular drive and focus, I would be twice as successful now.

3

CHARLIE

The tower crane turned with the grace of an oversized falcon hovering over the top of the construction site and began its descent down to pick up more plywood.

A cluster of fluffy white clouds shifted enough to block the sunlight, taking not only the light, but also the warmth with it, leaving a noticeable chill in the air.

The rumbling roar of a cement drill not six feet away blocked out any other sounds.

Jack, my intern, handed me a pen without looking in my direction.

Jack, I was quickly learning was one of the best. I'd snagged him on his final internship from Louisiana Tech. Any interns from Tech were automatically the best. Of course, I could be a bit biased, graduating from Louisiana Tech myself.

I'd say I had made quite a bit of progress in the past eight years. I'd been on the cover of Engineering News-Record along with three other young engineers as "ones to watch."

That article had been synergistic with the strides I was already making in the industry. After that, it had almost been like watching my career move of its own accord. Things had leveled out now, of course, but I was in a good place.

Noah Worthington had sought me out personally to oversee this building. Since I was an independent contractor, it had turned out to be my most lucrative job to date.

I'd always been loyal only to myself, but it hadn't taken long for Noah to gain my admiration.

He was an exemplary business man—one that I sought to emulate.

I checked my watch. If I left now, I wouldn't have to worry about being late for my appointment with Noah.

Another thing drilled into my head by my father. *If you're on time, you're late.*

"I'll come by tomorrow," I said to Jack.

"Take care," Jack said, with a companionable slap on the back, probably relieved to have me out of his hair for the rest of the day. I certainly remembered my internship days. Hard to function with the supervisor standing over your shoulder watching your every move.

Not that I did, but... I kind of did. It was just natural. After all, I was the one responsible at the end of the day.

Retracing my steps, I headed across the open floor, stepped onto the creaky elevator, my singular focus set on getting to my Mercedes parked across the street.

I reached the first floor and the elevator door slowly rumbled open. I instinctively wrapped my fingers around my key fob. Didn't need to even touch it. The locks would open automatically when I got three steps away from the car.

My new model Mercedes-AMG GT was in my sight and my head was already there.

The bright sun was out again and I was actually looking forward to the drive north of Houston to the airport. Driving meant I wasn't required to do anything except think my own thoughts. I could make phone calls if I wanted to... or not.

Opening my phone, I punched in the address to Skye Travels into my GPS, not because I needed help getting there, but so that I could gauge my time.

The airport was north of Houston and traffic determined my route from several choices.

I chose the most direct route which also happened to have the least amount of traffic and sent it to my car.

Still looking down at my phone, I walked straight into someone, eliciting an oomph. I instinctively put out a hand to keep whoever I had just slammed into from falling.

My arms wrapped around a decidedly feminine form.

I knew full well that there were no women on site, but I knew even more a female form when I felt one against me.

In this sea of construction working men, I found it significant that she smelled like a field of wildflowers.

Definitely a female.

Annoyed that one of the workers had brought his wife on site—and without a hard hat at that—I straightened, ready to fire someone.

Construction sites were dangerous by nature. Even without codes and guidelines to follow, they were not a place for family.

"Watch where you're going," she said, beating me to the punch.

"You're the one who ran into me," I said.

She stepped aside, pulling away from me in obvious annoyance.

"Is that so?" she asked, pulling herself to her full height. Even on three-inch heels, she was still a head shorter than me. Who wore three-inch heels to a construction site anyway?

"What are you doing here?" I asked, taking in her appearance. Other than not wearing a hardhat, she looked nothing at all like I expected one of my workers wives to look like.

She was dressed in a professional black jacket and skirt. A white button-down shirt. Heels. And her brunette hair was long, sleek, and straight.

Her features were angelically perfect. It only took an instant to take in her siren green eyes framed with long, dark lashes, a heart shaped face with creamy smooth skin, and red lipstick that instantly reminded me of the 1940s, though I have no reason why since I obviously had no experience with anything related to the 1940s.

And she held a clipboard similar to mine, without the scuffs.

And then I knew who she was.

"You're early," I said.

4

MAKENNA

The construction site was like any other.

Probably a hundred men wearing yellow hardhats, over half of them standing around, talking bullshit, the other half doing the actual work.

It was a widely accepted phenomenon that looked worse than it was. So many legitimate reasons.

They all had their specialty areas whether it was welding or running a jackhammer or driving a crane.

The most important reason, for some of them at least, was probably so that if one man got into trouble, there would be others around to help.

Safety first. No matter the cost.

My Grandpa Noah had drilled that into my head since I was a kid. With Grandpa being a pilot, he put safety before anything else. No matter what.

From the tires on the airplane to the correct amount of fuel to the weather.

Details.

I learned the importance of details from sitting on his lap in the cockpit of a small jet.

Never went into the air, though, without first being buckled into a six-point harness. In retrospect, I'm surprised he didn't have me wearing a hardhat, too.

The soft breeze carried the scent of diesel fuel and a fine mist of concrete dust that would leave a coating on my Chanel jacket and skirt by the time I left here.

Grandpa had a good instinct for hiring the best and apparently the engineer he had hired for this job was one of those best.

I made a couple of notes on my clipboard, but everything I was seeing was up to my green energy standards.

This was the way I liked to work. Slipping in and out without anyone noticing.

I stood still for a minute, watching the men work. Listening.

The beeping of a concrete truck as it backed up. The shrill rattling vibration of cement drills. Loud masculine voices.

One man shouted something indiscernible that was followed a burst of male laughter.

It never ceased to amaze me how a skyscraper or even a mid-rise building like this went up from nothing more than an idea. One of my cousins was an architect and I was fascinated by the whole process. Not enough that I wanted to make a career out of it, but fascinated nonetheless.

The wind brought a whiff of cigarette smoke, jarring me out of my reverie.

Ready to leave now, I turned around and slammed headlong into one of the men.

"Oomph."

I wasn't in danger of falling. At least I didn't think so. I never had a chance to find out.

Caught in a masculine vise and held firmly against a hard masculine chest.

I had the fleeting, nonsensible thought that he didn't *smell* like a construction worker. He smelled earthy, but beneath it, he smelled like expensive men's cologne.

I should have been paying attention. *He* should have been paying attention.

I was not only annoyed, I was embarrassed.

"Watch where you're going," I said, choosing to let the annoyance win and straightening, but his hold on me was tight.

"You ran into me," he said, with indignance. I noted that his voice was smooth as silk, despite the obvious irritation that ran through it.

"Is that so?" I asked, taking a step away from him and turning to face him.

"What are you doing here?" he asked, looking at me with one of those head to toe sweeping gazes that was quick and assessing.

He was dressed in a professional charcoal business suit with a light layer of cement dust giving it a shimmering hue. A white button-down shirt. His dark hair was short and barely grazed his collar. He was clean-shaven with classic movie star features.

His eyes, after they finished their sweep of my appearance locked onto mine. His were a deep blue that were annoyingly sparkly.

Not only was he vexingly handsome, he was wearing a white hardhat. And carrying a clipboard that had seen better days.

This was not one of the workers.

I had run headlong into someone who was definitely not a regular construction worker.

"You're early," he said.

"Early?" I shook my head and made a face. "Early for what?"

The rumbling roar of cement drills mixed with the sounds of men shouting. And the clinking of metal against metal ran through it all.

"No matter," he said. "Who let you in without a hat?"

I crossed my arms over my clipboard, holding it close. "I let myself in."

He narrowed his eyes as he studied me. Then he nodded and held out a hand. "I'm Charlie Alexander, Project Engineer."

I looked at him, then shook his hand. It would just be rude to do otherwise.

"Come on," he said. "We have a meeting."

"Okay," I said, totally confused. Somehow Charlie Alexander, Project Engineer, knew who I was. I was pretty sure I had never met him.

And yet, he'd introduced himself, so he didn't think we knew each other.

I shook my head.

He was already walking toward the door that led out to the road. I followed, my heels clicking on the concrete, refusing to rush to catch up with him.

"You can ride with me," he said, stopping until I was almost caught up with him.

What the—?

"I have my own car," I said, matter-of-factly, ignoring the glance he shot in my direction.

We reached the framed-out door and walked through. I found it a little amusing that he walked through the door frame when he could just as easily have walked through one of the framed-out walls.

On the street now, he stopped and looked at me.

A late model car and an SUV passed on the road behind him. One of the concrete trucks moved, its deep motor rumbling and clattering as it pulled out of the dirt parking lot behind us.

I lifted an eyebrow and waited.

I thought I saw the shadow of a smile cross his features, but I might have been mistaken.

"We have a meeting with Noah Worthington at Skye

Travels," he said, pulling his cell phone out of his inside jacket pocket.

I kept a straight face. At least I think I did. Didn't much matter. He wasn't looking at me now. He was looking down at his phone.

"Give me your number and I'll text you the address."

"I have the address," I said, not moving.

Now he was looking at me sideways. "Are you sure?"

"Skye Travels at the airport?"

"Yes." He put one hand on his hip.

I rattled off the address.

"Good enough," he said with a shrug. "Meet you there."

I watched him stride away. He definitely strode. Straight to his silver Mercedes sedan.

He got into the driver's seat, waited about two seconds, then pulled out onto the road heading to San Felipe.

I made a sound. I wasn't sure if it was a scoff or a laugh. Maybe a little of both.

Walking in the other direction, I got into my Bentley Continental GT.

Black.

Not silver. Black.

5

CHARLIE

By the time I pulled into the Skye Travels parking lot, I was in a foul mood.

It may have been ten years since I'd been home, but I called my parents every Sunday evening. I prided myself that they could set their clocks by it.

My sister had been home, several times, but sometimes she went weeks without calling. At least I called on a regular basis. I figured that made up for not visiting in what was probably a twisted kind of way, but it kept my guilt at bay.

Since I stayed in touch, they never called me, except for birthdays and Christmas. They respected my work. They knew I was busy.

By the time I left the construction site and reached my car, my phone was vibrating. My mother calling from her cell phone.

A bolt of panic shot through me, twisting my gut with dread. Only one thought consumed my brain. This was that call I had been dreading. One of two. Either a call from my mother or a call from my father.

This one just happened to be from my mother. The call that

something had happened to my father. I knew it was going to happen one day. I just didn't want it to be *now*.

Logically I knew there would never be a good time, but why couldn't it just be later?

My fear, though, was ill-founded. Thank God.

With the residual fear still coursing through my veins, it had been hard to pay attention to my mother's words after I realized that she was not calling to tell me that my father had died or was otherwise incapacitated.

The gist of the conversation had led to a heap of guilt dumped over my head.

Your father and I aren't getting any younger.

Maybe you could come home this year for Christmas.

We really miss you. And we're getting old.

I listened, quietly mostly, all the way to the airport.

"I have to go, Mom," I said. "I'm pulling into a meeting. I'll call you Sunday."

As we disconnected, I parked the car and sat quietly, taking a minute to compose myself.

My mother had caught me completely off guard. She'd called me during the day—a workday. And my heart was still racing with dread.

It was stupid.

But for all my avoidance of going home to Whiskey Springs, I love my parents. I loved them in spite of everything.

So while I was dealing with the shock of her calling me out of the blue like that—not quite Christmas or a birthday, she'd poured guilt onto me. Just like pouring hydrogen peroxide over an open wound. It burned and bubbled and hurt like hell.

I slid my phone back into my pocket. Besides, like guilt, hydrogen peroxide had been shown to be detrimental to wounds and relationships respectively.

Taking a deep breath, I tucked it all away. I had a meeting

with Noah Worthington. I could not afford to be distracted by parental guilt about not visiting my parents for Christmas.

I'd already opened the door and stepped out before I remembered that my assistant… what was her name? I didn't even remember her name. I was usually better about remembering names, but my brain was scrambled. At any rate, my new administrative assistant, who had shown up for work three weeks early, must have gotten lost. *She had the address.* Or was stuck in traffic, most likely.

I would worry about her later. Right now I needed to put all my focus on my meeting.

Since I had been here before, I knew right where to go. I went in through the front door and pressed the elevator button.

If the girl had given me her number, I could have called to check on her. But she was a stubborn one. I'd known her all of two minutes, maybe less, and I already knew that about her.

I didn't mind. She had looked amazing on paper.

The elevator door opened and I stepped inside.

It was probably not a good thing that I noticed how amazing she looked *in person.*

It was not that kind of relationship.

I never mixed work and pleasure.

Been there and done that. Had the t-shirt.

It never ended well.

Still. I wouldn't complain about having someone pretty to look at while I worked.

I stepped out of the elevator onto the second floor where the Skye Travels logo had been boldly painted across the wall. I turned left and received a go-ahead nod from the receptionist.

I walked through the empty waiting area toward the suite of offices. The waiting area did not look like a waiting area. It looked like five, maybe six, little living rooms each with its own chandeliers and gas fireplaces. Each one had a sofa and a couple of chairs. A television. A big desk with plenty of workspace.

And somehow each of the rooms had a floor to ceiling view of the tarmac. Someone had done an excellent job with their design.

A glass walled conference area was at the end of the short hallway. I turned left.

The generous use of glass made the small space seem larger than it was. And definitely more open than it was.

I reached Noah's office and stopped at his open door. His office had both a large desk and a seating area with two comfortable arm chairs with an end-table between them. He had two bottles of water on the end-table.

He was standing at the window, also floor to ceiling, staring outside, his hands behind his back.

The man was probably nearing seventy years old, but he didn't look a day over fifty. A handsome, well-dressed man. The epitome of success.

He turned. "Come in, Charlie," he said with a sweep of his hand and a lopsided grin. "Take a seat."

"My assistant is right behind me," I said. *I think.*

Noah pressed a button on his desk. "If Mr. Alexander's assistant shows up, please show her... or him... to the conference room."

I sat in one of the arm chairs, picked up a bottle of water, and drank deeply.

By the time Noah joined me in the chair kitty-corner from mine, my nerves were sufficiently settled.

"I need your help with something," Noah said.

"Of course. Anything you need."

I set my bottle of water down and waited for Noah to explain what it was he needed. It was no doubt something with the layout of the building. I just hoped he didn't want to do something crazy, but not unheard of, like add an extra floor.

But sometimes that happened. After people saw what they were getting, they started to think about other things they could do to make it even better.

"I need you to go to Whiskey Springs," Noah said with a lopsided grin.

6

MAKENNA

I parked in the little Skye Travels parking lot. I'd parked here a hundred times before. In fact, I remember the days before this parking lot was even covered. But now it was more of a covered garage. Helped combat both rainy and the worst of the hot weather, both almost all but necessary in Houston, especially since most of the people who parked here drove luxury cars.

With the private terminal being so close to the tarmac, the smell of jet fuel was strong, and there was a constant roar of airplanes taking off and landing overhead.

I was surprised that there were only three cars parked in the garage right now. Four with mine. Grandpa's. The receptionist.

And a silver Mercedes sedan.

Seeing the silver Mercedes sent an unexpected little shiver along my spine.

Very unexpected.

I'd spent the drive up here, trying to figure out just what was going on with Charlie Alexander, Building Engineer.

He seemed to think he knew who I was.

It was possible, very likely in fact, that he had spoken with my grandfather about me going out to take a look around the building site.

Charlie wouldn't have recognized me because we'd never met.

That was the only logical explanation.

I turned off the motor and stepped out of the car. Stretched. The drive, really, seemed to be getting worse. More congested. I liked it that Grandpa had decided to build an office for himself closer to his house.

He had drivers available at any time, but he had a tendency to get in his car at random times and drive himself up to the airport. Old habits died hard and all that.

I walked past the silver Mercedes, peeking inside as I passed. The car was clean. Nothing inside. Not even an empty coffee cup or water bottle. Nothing personal in sight. Perhaps I could add OCD to my impression of Charlie Alexander.

I hadn't completely formed my opinion of him. He had been rather abrupt and not much of a gentleman. I didn't know much—anything—about him, but it seemed like I had read somewhere or someone had told me that he was from out west.

He'd basically instructed me to follow him, then left me standing on the side of the road. He was no Texas cowboy gentleman. That was for sure.

It was quite baffling.

If he had been going anywhere other than my grandfather's office at Skye Travels, I wouldn't have followed him here. But Skye Travels was like a second home.

I went in through the door and pressed the elevator button.

Besides, I was curious.

He had acted rather rude and abrupt, yet professional at the same time. Professional, considering that he had slammed right into me and grabbed hold, catching me with strong arms. I'd been close enough to find out that he smelled good.

The elevator opened and I got off on the second floor. It was quiet here in the Skye Travels offices.

I saw no sign of Charlie, so he was probably already in with my Grandpa.

"Good morning, Makenna," Betty, the receptionist said with a big smile. Betty had been with Skye Travels since before I left for college, so she had been working at that desk for over ten years.

Betty had blonde hair, in a perfect blunt bob. She'd worn it that way as long as I'd known her.

"Good morning, Betty," I said. "How's the new grandbaby?"

Betty lowered her black-rimmed glasses and beamed. "Beautiful," she said. Then added excitedly. "I have pictures."

"Pictures." I hurried over to stand next to her behind her desk. "Let's see them."

Betty's desk had three large computer monitors lined up in front of her. The middle one had today's schedule on it. The one on the left had a red Skye Travels logo screensaver bouncing around the screen. The one on the right had some kind of Excel document on it.

Betty's desk was clutter-free. Just one yellow legal pad and a pen and her personal cell phone.

I spent the next ten minutes gushing over Betty's one-year-old grandbaby. He was kinda cute, but he looked like a handful to me.

"Thanks for sharing, Betty," I said, giving her a quick hug. "I'm gonna head back and find Grandpa."

"Sure," Betty said. "But… you might want to give him a minute. He's got somebody in there with him."

I glanced over my shoulder toward the hallway. "Charlie Alexander, Engineer?"

Betty smiled, her eyes twinkling with mischief. "That's the one." Then she tilted her head to the side questioningly. "How did you know that?"

I shrugged. "That is actually a good question."

She blinked once, then pinned my gaze with her piercing brown eyes, not taking my vague statement for an answer.

"He was at the construction site when I dropped by," I explained.

Betty nodded and lowered her voice. "He's kind of good looking."

"I didn't notice," I said with a little lift of one eyebrow.

Betty laughed. "You, my dear, are not as blind as you pretend to be."

I bent down and whispered. "He thinks I'm someone else."

"Who—" Betty grinned. Then held up a finger. "Ah. I know."

"What?" I glanced over my shoulder again.

"Hold on," Betty said when the phone rang, put on her headset, and scheduled a flight for a client for the morning.

Then she seamlessly turned back to me. "Were you supposed to meet him here?"

"Yes," I said, frowning. "It's really the oddest thing."

"Not so odd," Betty said, then added in a whisper. "He thinks you're his administrative assistant."

"His... what? Why?"

"I don't know why, but he does."

"That's just the silliest..." I straightened, about to go set Charlie Alexander straight.

"Wait," Betty said, putting a hand on my arm. "This might be fun," she said.

I shook my head. "I don't see—"

Putting her glasses back on, Betty turned to the computer screen on her left, typed in her password and pulled up her email.

About two seconds later, she turned back to me. "There," she said, tapping a well-manicured finger on the screen.

"Margaret Gray."

I leaned forward, peering at her computer. Right in an

email, Betty had correspondence between Grandpa and Charlie hiring one Margaret Gray as his executive administrative assistant. Starting January 3.

"He said I was early," I murmured, to myself, straightening.

Betty nodded sagely. "There you go. He thinks you're Margaret Gray."

"Well," I said, "I'm not."

Betty turned around, looking me dead in the eyes.

"Makenna," she said, thoughtfully. Then nodded.

"What?" I asked, suspicious of that look in her eyes. I'd seen it before.

"Be Margaret," she said. "No. Be *Maggie*."

I was already shaking my head. I didn't know what she was suggesting, but whatever it was, it could not possibly bode well for me.

Betty glanced over my shoulder. "Noah is sending Charlie to Whiskey Springs."

"Why?" I interrupted.

"He's got that airport project thing," she said quickly, waving my question away with a hand. "Go with him."

I looked blankly at her.

"I don't think this is a good idea."

"What else do you have planned for the weekend?"

"I…" I crossed my arms and thought. I thought really hard. I had been planning to go for a long jog. Rewatch Bridgertons on Netflix. Do some Christmas shopping.

Betty looked at me with that piercing gaze again.

"I have to do some Christmas shopping," I said.

Betty turned around in her chair, tapped the keyboard to silence her beeping computer screen, then turned back.

"Do it later. Or do it there. But go. Be Maggie for a weekend. What could it possibly hurt?"

I opened my mouth, then closed it.

It could possibly hurt everything.

She'd said herself that Charlie was good looking.

I did not need trouble.

But… she was right about one thing. I didn't exactly have anything planned.

"I don't know anything about being an administrative assistant," I said, trying to keep the peevishness out of my voice.

Betty made a face at me. "Who handles all your scheduling and office duties?"

"I do it all myself," I said. "I don't have anyone—"

"Exactly," Betty said, raising her hands in a rest my case gesture.

I had one more defense.

"Is my brother in Whiskey Springs?" I asked. "Or is he on his way home already? Because if he's there…"

"He should be on his way here," she said, glancing at the calendar on her computr and smiling brightly. "But you never know about him."

I nodded slowly.

Betty was far too quick to jump on that. I knew that my brother was coming here for Christmas, I just didn't know when exactly.

As a blonde, Betty had different thought patterns than I did as a brunette.

Biting my bottom lip, I considered this.

Even as I considered it, I knew. I just knew that Betty was going to get me into trouble.

7

CHARLIE

I left Noah's office feeling a little bit dazed.

The man was sending me *home* for Christmas. And he didn't even know it. I had not told him and I honest to God didn't think he even realized that I was from Whiskey Springs.

I couldn't remember if that had ever even come up in conversation. I would have bet money that it had not. It wasn't something I went around telling people, so I'd remember if I we had talked about it.

But he could have found out. The man could find out anything he wanted. It would have shown up when he did a background check which I had no doubt he would have done. Any smart man would have. And Noah was brilliant.

I walked out of his office, down the hallway, past the glass-walled conference room, down another hall until I reached the waiting area.

The receptionist looked up and smiled at me over her glasses before she beckoned me over. According to her nameplate, her name was Betty. Betty was a middle-aged professional looking woman, exactly the kind of person I would expect Noah to hire as his assistant.

Noah was a married man, so no young, tempting eye candy at the office. Just a professional, settled woman. I smiled to myself. Noah's wife was a psychologist, so she'd probably had something to do with the hiring.

"Your assistant, Margaret Gray, is waiting," Betty said with a nod in the general direction of the main waiting area.

Margaret. So that was the girl's name. I remembered now. It had been in the thread of emails that I had barely glanced at.

Margaret sat on a small sofa a few feet in front of Betty's receptionist desk, just outside of the waiting areas for clients.

I was again struck by how pretty she was. Brunette hair flowing past her shoulders in soft waves.

She looked up at me with a smile that had me nearly missing a step.

"Margaret," I said. "Thank you for waiting."

"Not a problem." She stood up. "You can call me Maggie."

"Right," I said. "Maggie."

"You said we had a meeting," she said, her smile turning a bit lopsided. Why did that look vaguely familiar?

"Yes," I said. "Wasn't what I'd expected. Can you and I meet for a few minutes?" I asked. "How about...?"

I glanced back at Betty questioningly. "Can we use one of these waiting rooms?"

"Absolutely," she said with a sure nod. "Go right ahead."

Maggie followed me over to sit in one of the waiting rooms. We each sat in one of the armchairs.

The flames from the gas fireplaces burned brightly. I vaguely wondered if they ran the air conditioning while they ran the fireplace.

Would not surprise me, but it was still a nice touch.

I glanced at my watch. I needed to be back downtown in one hour.

"I apologize," I said, "but I have to be straight and to the point."

"I understand," she said, with a little lift of one eyebrow.

"I appreciate you coming to work early," I said. "And it's good timing."

"How so?"

I took a deep breath. I still couldn't believe I was doing this. It felt surreal. Ten years. Ten years since I had been back there.

"I…we… need to go to Whiskey Springs to check out an airport terminal Mr. Worthington is building."

"I see," she said, sitting back in her chair. I couldn't read her blank expression.

I found myself holding my breath, waiting for her to tell me she wasn't available. I hadn't considered until this very moment, that she might not actually be here for work just yet. Maybe she had just been checking things out. After all, she had just moved from… somewhere.

"I'll pay you, of course."

She lifted an eyebrow and if it hadn't been ludicrous, I would have sworn she looked offended.

Apparently my brain was still scrambled.

"When do we leave?" she asked calmly.

"In the morning," I said. "If you'll give me your number, I'll text you the information. I actually have to get with Betty…"

She reached into her handbag. "I'll give you my card," she said, then stopped, looking over at Betty. "Actually I just remembered I don't have any cards yet."

I pulled one of my own business cards out of my wallet and handed it to her.

"Thank you," she said and wrote her number on the back of my card along with her name.

As she handed me the card, our fingers brushed and I was immediately reminded of how she had felt against me. Soft and feminine.

I belatedly—very belatedly—realized that I should have followed Noah Worthington's lead and hired a middle-aged married woman who didn't scramble my thoughts at a mere touch.

Especially one without that megawatt smile that needed to come with a high voltage danger warning.

"Thank you," I said. "I'll let you get back to whatever you were doing. I'll text you the information, but plan on leaving in the morning unless you hear differently."

"Sure thing, Mr. Alexander," she said turning that smile on me again before she headed out.

I waited until she reached the elevator before I trusted myself to stand up and walk back over to stand in front Betty.

"Everything okay?" Betty asked, jarring my attention away from watching Maggie as she stepped onto the elevator.

"Everything is great," I said, looking at Betty now. "Noah wants us to head to Whiskey Springs in the morning."

"Yes, he does," she said, then. "She seems like a nice girl."

I nodded. "She's my new assistant." I bit back the smile that nearly burst across my face.

Betty turned away and I thought I saw the shadow of a smile cross her features, but I probably imagined it. "I know," she said. "Pull that chair over here and have a seat. Let's work out this schedule."

After absently dragging a straight backed chair over to the counter beside her, I let out a breath.

This was going to be interesting.

Not only was I going home for the first time in ten years, I was taking my new assistant. My new gorgeous assistant.

Life was a funny thing indeed.

8

MAKENNA

The thing about living on the twenty-fourth floor of an apartment building was that I rarely saw birds.

A flock of birds fluttered upwards together in a clump and settled in the bare branches of trees in a little park below.

It was kinda odd always being above the birds. I'd never seen them fly this high.

And the rain was a whole different story. Rain did not *look* like rain this high up. There was no patter or splashing on the ground. Just a general haziness. Unless, of course, there was a thunderstorm. Then the lightning could be seen from miles away. Lightning shows were quite astounding from up here.

My hands on my hips, I stared at the open suitcase on my queen-sized bed and sipped from my glass water bottle.

My *empty* open suitcase.

I had several stacks of clothes laid out on the bed, but I had no idea what to pack.

What did one pack for a couple of days, what was essentially a weekend away, even if it was during the week, with a man—a good-looking man—who thought he was my boss?

When one was pretending to be an assistant named Maggie Gray?

I'd never been an assistant, unless I counted my internship in college. Even then my supervisor had pretty much given me free rein.

I'd been in the top ten percent of my class at Yale. Then I'd gone on to get my MBA. A side-effect of being one of the top students in my class was that I had not played. While classmates were out partying, I was in my apartment. Studying.

At twenty-six, I had never had a serious boyfriend. Just casual dates. The occasional pizza and movie nights I'd had tended to be with family.

It didn't worry me. I was of the mind that when it was time I would find the person that I was supposed to be with.

I rolled up two pairs of jeans and put them in the suitcase.

There. A person always needed jeans when traveling out of town.

It was a start anyway and seemed to break the damn. I added in two pairs of sleep pants and three t-shirts. A sweatshirt.

I had cousins who pushed me to sign up for dating sites, but that seemed too fake to me.

Call me old-fashioned, but I wanted to meet someone the way my grandparents had. Face-to-face. Out of the blue. Cupid's arrow making its mark and all that.

Charlie Alexander's image flashed through my mind and I shoved it away with annoyance.

Charlie Alexander was not that someone.

I'd been crazy to let Betty talk me into this.

For about the hundredth time, I thought about calling him. Telling him there had been a big misunderstanding and I was not his assistant.

Then I never had to see him again. He would never have to know that my real name wasn't Maggie.

But since I hadn't heard from him yet, I didn't have his phone number.

And blast it if Betty wasn't right. It had been a long time since I had done anything just for fun.

As far as dangerousness went, it was on the minimal side.

I probably wouldn't make it very long into the trip before I blew it anyway. I had almost blown it today when I had reflexively reached into my handbag for a business card.

No. I was pretty sure I wasn't going to make it very long before I blew my cover.

I didn't know how I was going to fix everything when that invariably happened .

Just confess that I wanted a weekend away. Oh. That would go over like a ton of bricks.

It was stupid.

I went to stand in my closet and looked at my dresses.

Worst case, Grandpa would send someone to get me. All I had to do was to say the word and he would send a private jet for me. It was what he did. Other people sent cars. He sent jets.

I grabbed my favorite little black dress off the hanger, folded it, and dropped it into the suitcase.

An assistant would need business clothes. But we were going to the mountains. In the winter.

I dragged a pair of wool slacks off the hanger, put them in the suitcase along with the jacket and a long-sleeve silk blouse.

Checked my phone again.

I should have heard from Charlie by now. It was a quarter to nine. He wasn't going to text me tonight. Probably forgot or didn't think it was important enough.

I decided he wasn't the most considerate person I'd ever met.

Definitely not someone I wanted to date.

I was just going to Whiskey Springs to… to see my brother.

And yes, I agreed with myself. I could do that anytime I wanted to. I did not have to stowaway as someone's assistant.

Maybe I would just give Betty a stocking full of coal for Christmas this year.

She was a very bad influence.

Very bad.

I wondered if my grandfather knew what she had put me up to.

Deciding there was no way she would tell him that, I decided to wear my tall black boots. The ones without the heels. They went with everything. Jeans. Suits. Dresses.

Having lived in Connecticut for five years, I knew a little bit about dressing for cold weather, even if it didn't come naturally. I was a Houston girl, born and bred.

Deciding I would spend the rest of the evening having a glass of red wine and watching television or maybe do some reading, I dragged the suitcase off my bed. I could finish my clothing selection in the morning.

Since I had not heard from Charlie, I would have to be up early.

Blast it all.

Enough with all this.

I sent Betty a quick text. She had gotten me into this. She could be disturbed.

ME: *What time is our flight in the morning?*

As she answered me with thought bubbles, I poured myself a glass of wine and curled up on my ever so comfortable sofa with the novel I was reading.

There were definite advantages to being single and living alone.

9

CHARLIE

The next morning I pulled into the Skye Travels one-story garage and parked my Mercedes across from a black pick-up truck, a white Toyota Camry, and a black Bentley Continental GT.

The weather today was beautiful. More like September in the mountains than how I thought December should be. But this was Houston and the weather tended toward the warm side, at least until January and February. Two months of winter was about all we got down here.

I didn't mind the warmth of the sun coming through my windshield as I had fought traffic to get here.

I didn't mind the breeze either that held a hint of chill as it carried the scent of jet fuel across the tarmac.

The Bentley, I decided as I walked past it, belonged to someone with family money, probably a young couple heading up to Montana for Christmas. Old money or new money didn't much matter. They had the money to spend their Christmas jaunting off to the mountains on a private jet.

I, too, was jaunting off to the mountains on a private jet, but I was going for work.

After a moment's hesitation, I decided to leave my suitcase in the trunk for now.

As I stepped inside the building and pushed the up button on the elevator, I reminded myself that I could take a holiday on a private jet if I wanted to.

I'd grown up in a small town. A very small town in the mountains. And my family was conservative.

Despite having the money to fly first class, my parents flew coach the few times they'd traveled. But even that was a very rare thing for them to do. They both insisted that they lived in the most beautiful place in the country. So why would they travel anywhere else?

Coming from a conservative background, to me it seemed a bit extravagant to fly private. But Noah insisted.

I had sent Maggie a text late last night giving her our flight time, but I hadn't heard back. Granted, I had texted late, but I had gotten busy on a project and had put it off a little too long, so it was my fault, all in all.

Fortunately, it had been too late for me to cave in to my impulse to call her when she didn't respond.

Pulling my cell phone out of my pocket, I checked again to see if she had responded.

Nothing.

Stubborn. That's what she was. If she didn't want to come along, then that was just fine.

"Good morning," Betty said as I stepped off the elevator and headed across the lobby. "Your plane will be ready in about..." She glanced at one of her three computer screens. "Fifteen minutes."

"Thank you," I said. That would put the plane right on time. Curious, I wandered to the window and looked down.

A sleek little jet sat there gleaming in the sunlight. The red Skye Travels logo splashed across the fuselage. A couple of techs walked around with iPads, checking off boxes.

Then I saw her.

Maggie, her long brunette hair tousled from the breeze, stood on the tarmac below, not far from the building's back door. Pacing back and forth, her head down, she stared at her phone, her fingers moving swiftly over the keys.

She paused and looked up, staring straight ahead and I felt a sucker punch to my gut.

She was beautiful. Stunningly gorgeous.

Dressed for winter, she wore a long black wool coat. She had two medium suitcases waiting nearby.

This was not a good idea. I should not have brought her on this trip.

I was drawn to her with every fiber of my being.

Not the best way to start off a working relationship.

She looked down and started pacing again, her fingers moving swiftly over the keys.

Stopping again, she smiled that megawatt smile at the tech who came over to take her suitcases to the plane.

It was stupid to feel jealous that she turned that smile on someone else so I turned away and took a deep, cleansing breath.

"Everything okay?" Betty asked, looking at me over her black-rimmed glasses.

"Everything is great," I said, forcing myself to smile back.

"I forgot to ask," she said. "Have you flown private before?"

Now how had she known that? What had I done to give myself away?

"No," I said. "Not really." Not at all, but a man had to have a little bit of pride.

"Well," Betty said. "You're going to love it. Everyone does. But just know, that once you fly with Skye Travels, you'll never be happy flying commercial again." She twirled back around and tapped on one of her keyboards.

"Right." I couldn't decide if Betty was just making

conversation or if she had some other reason for telling me this. Maybe this was just way of supporting her employers.

"Oh," she said, turning back. "And Maggie is waiting for you on the tarmac below."

"Thank you." I refused to tell her that I had already noticed. "I'll head down and grab my luggage." I hesitated. "Do I need to do anything else?"

"Nope," Betty said. "You're all set. Have a wonderful flight."

I felt off-kilter as the elevator took me back downstairs.

Nerves, maybe, I decided. But I'd never been a nervous flyer.

As much as I hated to admit it, the nerves were coming from seeing Maggie again. From knowing I was about to travel *home* with Maggie.

That was it. That was exactly what had me feeling off-center. Going to Whiskey Springs, for work, where I would see my family. *With Maggie.*

I was in a world of trouble.

All because of a cute little brunette with a megawatt smile.

10

MAKENNA

Today was a perfect day for flying. The warmth of the sun on my skin was offset by a cool breeze that tousled my hair. I swept a stray lock of hair out of my eyes and paced alongside the building.

I had gloves and a wool cap and a couple of scarves in my suitcases, but I wore my long wool coat. Packing for this trip had been challenging to say the least and even more challenging trying to pack winter clothes and everything that went with it into one suitcase, so I gave up and brought two.

I stood at the back of the Skye Travels building, on the tarmac, with the scent of jet fuel strong in the air. Having spent a lot of time here at my grandfather's office, I'd grown up with this familiar scent. One that I, oddly enough, found comforting.

Charlie Alexander... along with Betty... had thrown me for a loop.

I might not have had firm plans for the weekend, but I did have some responsibilities. For one I had to explain to my aunt why I suddenly wasn't able to take Sophia to her ice-skating lesson tomorrow.

My fingers flew over the keys as I texted my apology.

ME: *Something came up and I have to go out of town.*

AUNT AINSLEY: *Seriously? You never go anywhere.*

I stopped and glared at her message. Was that true? If so, when had that happened?

The minute I came back from Connecticut and started my consulting business.

ME: *I travel.*

A good thing text messages didn't convey tone.

AUNT AINSLEY: *Oh. It's business then. It's just...You usually have that planned ahead of time.*

I sighed. So she wasn't saying I never traveled so much as I wasn't spontaneous.

First of all, all Worthingtons travelled. It was in our DNA. So I'd known she was wrong about that.

But not being spontaneous couldn't possibly be much better than not traveling at all.

"Hello, Miss Fleming," Josh, one of the techs who had been looking over the airplane said as he came toward me. "Can I go ahead and load your luggage?"

"Of course," I said, giving him a smile.

He lowered his voice as he grabbed the handles on my suitcases. "Ms. Betty said we're to call you Miss Maggie Gray on this trip."

I laughed. "She did, did she?"

"Yes ma'am." He gave me a little wink. "Your secret is safe with me."

I didn't know whether to laugh or... run.

But I really didn't have the opportunity to do either before I looked up and saw Charlie coming through the gate, dragging his own suitcase. Only one, of course. It was different being a guy.

"Good morning," he said. He was dressed in a similar suit to what he had been wearing yesterday, except there was no layer of cement dust on his clothes today. And instead of a white button-down shirt, he was wearing a light blue one.

The light blue of his shirt brought out the blue of his eyes.

"Hi." I glanced back over at Josh. He grinned and tipped his hat.

Charlie followed my gaze, but by the time he caught sight of Josh, Josh had his back to us, arranging my suitcases in the plane's storage area.

"I guess you got my message," he said.

Hearing the twinge of annoyance in his voice, I smiled.

I could have let him know that I got his message, but since I hadn't gotten it until I woke up this morning, I'd let my own annoyance get in the way of good manners.

Besides, even as I'd rolled my luggage out to the car from my condo, I had not decided for sure that I was going to actually come.

I hadn't decided for sure until I'd stood on the tarmac and defended my lack of spontaneity to my aunt. As crazy as it was, that was my deciding factor.

I could be spontaneous when I wanted to be. I just hadn't wanted to be for a very long time.

"Right," I said, the smile still in place. "Thanks for the update."

I had expected him to completely miss my sarcasm, but he just smiled. The first time he had smiled at me.

My own smile faltered and I had to force it to stay in place. The man should really smile more often.

He was a handsome man already, even vexed with annoyance, but when he smiled, he looked downright gorgeous.

I swallowed hard. I would not fall prey to his charms.

This was a business trip.

I was his assistant, I reminded myself.

And my name was Maggie.
Maggie.
Right.
I could do this thing.
And I was going to have fun with it even if it killed me.

11

CHARLIE

The inside of the jet was larger than I had expected. It smelled like new leather. Much like a new car smell.

But it wasn't like on television with tables and couches. It was more like first class with three rows of two oversized seats separated by the aisle.

There were oval windows at each seat. All the shades were open, letting the sun stream inside.

The pilot—just one of them—sat with an iPad, going over a checklist, seemingly ignoring the radio chatter coming from the control tower and other pilots.

Personally, I would have found it distracting, but the pilot didn't seem to care. He'd introduced himself as Luke Worthington. One of Noah's boys—grandson to be precise.

What I could see of the cockpit from here looked dangerously complicated even for me and I'd used drafting software before.

Drafting software required only one computer screen. The cockpit had what looked from here like four screens, not counting all the different panels with a hundred buttons.

I suddenly felt like I had missed out on something by going into engineering and not aviation.

I always felt like that when I discovered something new and interesting. I tucked the idea into the back of my mind. Flying lessons.

And again, I reminded myself that I actually had the money to do it.

My parents had done nothing if they hadn't instilled in me a strong need for security.

Get a good job.

Save your money for retirement.

Something had always bothered me about that. My gut always told me to go with the whole seize the day philosophy. But that was in direct opposition to my upbringing.

Safe. Secure. Look before you leap.

My father was a small town physician, so I suppose he merely imparted the knowledge he had. Neither one of my parents were much of a risk taker.

It was a fight, getting past what they had ingrained in me over the years. Getting past that to my core instinct to be spontaneous and open to new things.

I sat in the front seat on the right. Maggie sat across from me on the left.

We had no flight attendant to tell us what to do, so I followed Maggie's lead.

After she easily fastened her four-point harness, she put her phone away and pulled a novel out of her handbag.

I was impressed at just how comfortable she seemed.

There might be more to Maggie Gray than met the eye as least as far as traveling went. She didn't seem the least bit confused or concerned about flying private.

I refused to let on that I was the least bit of a fish out of water.

As far as she was concerned, I did this all the time.

Sitting back in my chair, I watched her out of the corner of my eyes.

How did an executive administrative assistant become accustomed to flying on private jets?

I frowned at her and considered.

I should have taken some time to study her resume and learn about her, but I hadn't done that. I had just taken it for granted that she was like any other administrative assistant. Just prettier.

But on the contrary. She was like no administrative assistant I had met, much less worked for me.

I pulled out my phone and began searching my emails for the correspondence between me and Noah's office that hired Maggie as my personal executive assistant... sight unseen.

Other than what was on the paper, I knew nothing about her and to be honest, I hadn't paid much attention to that either. I had let Betty take care of it.

Well. That taught me to pay more attention.

Maybe she had worked for the Worthingtons before.

"Maggie," I said with every intention of getting a more indepth work history.

But she didn't answer me or even seem to hear that I was trying to talk to her.

Then she swept her hair back and touched her right ear.

Of course. The girl was wearing air pods. Listening to music, no doubt.

She had no idea I wanted to talk to her.

Blowing out a breath and shaking my head, I sat back in my chair and went back to looking for that email.

It was better this way anyway.

It was going to be a long enough flight with her just sitting there. It would be even longer if I had to look into her stunningly sparkling green eyes, especially if she turned that megawatt smile on me.

The plane was moving now, taxiing toward the runway, and the sunlight coming in through the window blinded me. I slid the shade closed over the window, sat back, and closed my eyes.

It wasn't like it mattered anyway, at this point.

Maggie was fully vetted and I was the one who had brought her along on this trip.

The plane stopped for a few minutes.

"Cleared for takeoff," the pilot announced in a quick blast of words that tumbled together as though he said them a thousand times a day.

Seconds later, we were moving again and the lights flickered just before the engine revved up, picking up speed.

Then we were in the air, the plane wobbling smoothly before leveling off.

I sneaked a peak over at Maggie. Her paperback lay open, face down on her lap and her eyes were closed.

She looked so serene. So calm.

Just as an executive assistant should look.

It wasn't her fault I couldn't take my eyes off of her.

12

MAKENNA

I sat across the aisle from Charlie in one of the two front leather chairs. Technically they were seats, but they were as comfortable as any chair.

The airplane's interior color scheme was called black piano. White leather with black trim. This was one of Grandpa's newest planes. I wasn't sure how we rated a trip on this one, but I wasn't one to complain.

This particular plane, the Embraer Phenom 300, still had that new car smell. Everything looked clean and untouched.

The monitors, which usually dropped from the ceiling, were still closed and I saw no need to open them for such a short flight. It would take just about two hours to get from Houston to the little airport of Whiskey Springs outside of Denver.

My cousin Luke was one of the best pilots.

Of course, I would have said that about any of the Skye Travels pilots, especially my uncles and cousins.

I closed the novel I had been pretending to read as Luke prepared for takeoff. Takeoff was the most exhilarating and nerve-wracking part of flying all at the same time. Since my brother was a pilot, too, I knew a little bit more than most people about the mechanics of flying.

Not only had my brother taken me up countless times, but I'd heard him studying with his friends, so I knew the ins and outs of the flying process. I'd also flown with Grandpa Noah and, of course, I'd flown with Luke before.

Between that and hanging out at the airport, I considered myself a veteran flyer.

I trusted Luke to get us off the ground safely, get us to Colorado, and back on the ground. That wasn't what troubled me.

What troubled me was the man sitting across from me.

Charlie had tried to talk to me before takeoff, but I'd pretended to be listening to music.

I was a fake book-reading fake music-listening fake Maggie Gray. Might as well take the fakeness all the way. If Charlie was going to talk to me, I was going to trip myself up because if he asked me anything other than basics I had studied about Maggie from the resume Betty had generously forwarded me, I would be lost.

I suppose I should take comfort in the fact that I knew about as much about Maggie Gray as he did.

Betty insisted that Charlie and Maggie had not met in person. No one had actually met Maggie and fortunately for me, she had no social media presence. Smart girl.

So I suppose that since I knew as much as he did, I could make up the rest.

It was possible, though, that he had spoken to her on the phone in person and no one knew it.

It was possible.

Although from what I was learning about him, it wasn't really all that likely. He seemed to be a take things as they came kind of guy.

I had memorized Maggie's resume. She and I had actually

started off with quite similar career paths, except that our paths had split off into different directions when I had gone on to get my MBA and start my own business. There was also the fact that I had gone to college at Yale and she had gone to the University of Houston.

We were both from Houston. It was just that I had been fortunate that I had family money that allowed me to take the risk to start my own business.

Not very many people, I would bet including Maggie Gray, did.

To my credit, I had succeeded and I no longer had to rely on my family for support. I took a great deal of pride in that.

At any rate, it seemed all I had to do was to stick with the facts I knew about her and fill in the rest with things from my own background.

I reached into my handbag and pulled out one of those soft mints in a seasonal cinnamony peppermint flavor.

Charlie Alexander looked decidedly uncomfortable, but I hadn't quite put my finger on what, exactly, he was uncomfortable about.

It didn't make him look any less appealing.

I caught him looking at me, his lips pursed in consternation, studying me as though he was trying to figure something out. That was in between his scrolling on his phone.

He crossed one leg over the other, then shifted a few minutes later, crossing the other leg.

Yes, I decided. He was most definitely uncomfortable.

Almost like a different man from the one I'd met at the construction site.

The one who had insisted that I follow him to the airport, then left me standing on the side of the street.

The plane leveled off, reaching high altitude, white fluffy clouds surrounding us.

It was stunningly beautiful.

A little smile on my face, I looked over at Charlie.

He was gripping the leather arms of the chair, his knuckles white. Staring out my window as we swept through the magnificent cloud bank. His window shade was closed.

At first I'd thought his expression was just blank, but upon closer inspection, I realized that he wasn't just staring blankly out the window.

He was afraid.

13

CHARLIE

I never would have classified myself as a nervous flyer.

But at the moment, for some reason, as the little airplane soared through the white fluffy clouds, I couldn't help thinking that no one could see anything.

I *knew* they had radar that could detect other planes. I *knew* that.

Maybe it was thinking about heading back to Whiskey Springs that had me out of sorts.

Maybe it was thinking about driving along a mountain side in the clouds. Not being able to see the side of the road, following nothing but the headlights of the car in front of me and hoping like hell that they didn't run over the edge. I shuddered to think about how many times that had happened.

I always figured that was a good time to just pull over and wait. Or avoid it altogether.

The pilot was most definitely not pulling over.

I jumped when Maggie put a hand on my arm.

"Hey," I said, trying to smile.

"Hey," she said, looking at me with a decidedly concerned expression. "Are you okay?"

"Yeah," I said. "Just not used to flying so low. In the clouds and all."

She nodded. "You know… this is an Embraer Phenom 300."

I shook my head. That meant absolutely nothing to me. "I don't really know airplanes."

She smiled now. That megawatt smile that had me forgetting my own name, especially with her sitting so close to me. She was close enough that I could smell the cinnamony peppermint in her mouth. Somehow she had slid her chair over next to mine.

I couldn't even begin to figure out how that could happen.

Reaching over and pressing a button on her console, she lowered a small screen about the size of an iPad from the ceiling.

"That image shows where we are," she said, then tapped another button, layering radar images over the screen. "We'll be out of the clouds in a few minutes."

I felt some of my nervousness dissipating as I watched the screen.

This was a fascinating airplane. And this was not driving through the clouds on the side of a mountain with no visibility.

But…

"How do you know so much about…?" I asked, waving a hand in a general direction. "This."

She opened her mouth to say something, then stopped as though she had changed her mind. "My brother's a pilot," she said, the words spilling out like a confession.

"Oh," I said. "That must be nice."

"Yeah, well," she said. "It could be, I guess, but he lives in another part of the country now."

"Where does he—?"

"And," she said, leaning over to press another button on her console. "If you get tired of watching the airplane which isn't very exciting, then you can watch a movie."

I watched as she pulled up Netflix.

"Wait," I said. "There's Wi-Fi on the plane?"

"Sure," she said. "There's guest Wi-Fi, so you can watch movies or use your phone or whatever."

"You weren't using your phone," I said.

She smiled a little. "I'm old-fashioned," she said. "I like to use flight time to reflect." She shrugged. "You know. Like the old days when there was no Wi-Fi on the planes."

I nodded. "Yes. I remember those days."

She smiled. And this time it wasn't that megawatt smile that I'd seen before. This smile was different. Warm and genuine. Soft.

I was enchanted.

"You've never flown private before," she said. It wasn't a question. It was simply a statement.

"What gave it away?" I asked, feeling a bit sheepish. Between her and Betty, I was starting to feel like an open book. I'd always considered myself decidedly constricted.

"I just have a sense about these things," she said. "But you needn't worry. As I'm sure you know, flying is much safer than driving."

I raised my window shade and looked outside just as the plane broke out of the clouds.

"I'm really not a nervous flyer," I said, wincing as the plane hit an air pocket and dropped a few feet.

"Okay." She gave me a patient smile now. One that she might give someone who had no idea what they were talking about.

I struggled to keep up with the vein of the conversation. I was much more intrigued by Maggie's different smiles. It seemed she had a different smile for just about anything.

"Just relax," she said, sitting back in her own chair and moving about to demonstrate relaxing.

Right. Now how exactly was I supposed to relax when her chair was still right next to mine. It would take no more than a little bit of turbulence for our shoulders to touch.

Relaxation was about the last thing on my mind right now.

Right now all I could think about was Maggie Gray.

14

MAKENNA

Even as I pretended to demonstrate relaxing, I was far from relaxed.

I should have just slid my leather chair back over to my side and started reading my book again. My book was a much, much safer bet.

The loud, smooth rumble of the engine should have been calming. Normally would have been calming. Except that it wasn't.

My heart was pumping the blood through my veins at a dangerous rate. So much so that my hands were shaking.

Despite my better judgement, I found myself replaying the way Charlie and I had met. The way his strong arms had felt around me. Even sitting here next to him, I could smell his intoxicating scent. Like expensive men's cologne. Earthy. Smoky. Like standing on the porch of a mountain cabin on a cool summer morning beneath dewy spruce and fir trees.

I swallowed thickly, then took a sip of my water and watched Charlie out of the corner of my eye. He barely flinched at the next air pocket.

Instead, he had pulled out his phone and started scrolling

again. Swallowing thickly, I took a deep breath and clasped my hands together in my lap.

"So you're from Houston," he said, glancing up from his phone.

Oh no. He was looking at Maggie's information. Probably her resume.

"Born and raised," I said with a little half smile. That one was easy. Both the real Maggie and I were from Houston.

Making a muffled sound, he went back to his phone. Even as I braced myself for more questions, I told myself that it was a good sign he was just now looking at *my*—Maggie's— information. That meant I was ahead of him.

"Are you originally from Houston?" I asked, trying to phrase the question so that I wasn't giving away what I did or did not know. I actually didn't have a clue where he was from. If I'd been smart, I would have looked him up last night, but convinced—almost convinced—myself that it didn't matter where he was from. That I didn't need to know anything about him. I was merely mollifying Betty... convincing her that I could be spontaneous... that I could be fun.

And there was Ainsley.

"Turbulence ahead. Fasten your seatbelts," Luke said over the speaker. The little ping of the fasten seatbelts sign followed.

Charlie glanced over at me, but he appeared to be fairly relaxed. No white-knuckled hold on the arm of the chair.

I checked my seatbelt to make sure it was secure, then braced myself. I was surprised Luke had said anything about turbulence. The Phenom was an exceptionally smooth aircraft. Besides that, it had built in mechanisms that automatically avoided air pockets. Or so I thought. Maybe he was just being cautious.

I reached into my handbag and pulled out the little tin of mints and opened it, releasing a cinnamon mint flavor. Held the open container out to him. "Want one?" I asked.

"Sure," he said, not meeting my gaze, taking one of the mints and absently popping it into his mouth.

I put the mints away and looked over at him sideways. "Is your seatbelt secure?"

"I'm sure it is," he said with a little shrug.

I started to tell him that turbulence was worse in small planes than large jets. I really was going to tell him that so he would be prepared.

But there was something about the set of his jaw that made me hesitate. He was keeping a wall around himself and I wasn't inclined to break down walls. Walls were there for a reason and it wasn't my job to tear them down.

Maybe the turbulence was something he just had to find out for himself.

I looked out the window at the perfectly clear blue sky. There would be mountains ahead, but I couldn't see them yet. Turbulence was definitely worse near the mountains.

I should just tell him.

Turning toward him, I put a hand on the arm of my chair which was only a couple of inches away from the arm of his chair. "You may not know this—"

When the turbulence hit, I stopped in mid-sentence. It felt like the plane dropped out from beneath us. No matter many times it happened… no matter how much I knew it was no big deal… it took my breath away.

Charlie grabbed my hand and held on for dear life.

Then just as quickly, the plane was flying smoothly again.

"That was rather—" he started to say something as we flew through another air pocket.

He squeezed my hand again.

"unexpected…." He finished his sentence and the plane leveled.

I had to agree.

Luke had been right. There had been turbulence in the air ahead.

The seconds ticked past. Neither one of us said anything. Neither one of us moved.

The turbulence seemed to have passed. Just as I thought it, the fasten seat belts light went off with a little pinging sound.

So all was clear.

There was just the roar of the engine. The plane indicator on the monitor had come back on, showing us that we were flying over Denver now. Already, I could feel the plane decreasing in altitude.

We would be in Whiskey Springs in no time.

We just sat there. And we were still holding hands.

It was one of those weird situations. The longer we sat here like this, the harder it was to pull away. It would be awkward to pull away and it was awkward to sit still, not pulling away.

15

CHARLIE

It should have been awkward.
Right?

Maggie and I sat in our chairs—technically seats, with the roar of the jet engine in the background as the plane began its descent into Whiskey Springs. We would be landing at the airport that was really little more than a runway. A short runway, but one I trusted the pilot would have no trouble successfully navigating.

I'd grabbed her hand when the plane fell out beneath us. I suppose that the sensation of dropping out of the sky was something a person got used to. Not sure it was something I would ever get used to or even want to.

I had never been a thrill-seeker heading off to ride the rollercoasters. One time. I had ridden a rollercoaster one time at the Mall of America on a trip with one of my friends in high school. I'd held it together until the rollercoaster came to a stop and after finally letting us off, I headed straight to the restroom. Then I had puked. That had been the one and only time I had ridden a rollercoaster.

Maybe I would just leave the piloting to those who liked this sort of adventure and stick to my building construction world.

I had grabbed Maggie's hand out of reflex. At least that was what I told myself.

Then I hadn't wanted to let go. And she hadn't pulled away.

Somehow it felt so right. So very right.

How could something that felt so right be wrong?

In my defense, neither one of us moved.

So we sat here, side by side, holding hands as the seconds ticked past and the plane descended toward the airport.

The leather chairs were comfortable enough to have easily been in someone's living room. I crossed one leg over my other knee and made an effort to relax my shoulders.

Once we landed, a car would be waiting for us in Whiskey Springs. Noah had seen to that.

It was so very odd. Noah sending me to take a look at a job in my hometown.

I hadn't told Maggie that I was from Whiskey Springs. It hadn't seemed necessary since she was my executive assistant. Not my girlfriend.

It did seem like something an assistant would know, though, didn't it?

I had no doubt that Betty knew where Noah was from. Probably knew a great deal about his history as well as his personal life. It was just natural to know the people you worked for.

As I sat there, my hand clasped tightly with hers—it was possible that Maggie couldn't have pulled away even if she'd wanted to—I felt the boundary between assistant and something more personal slipping.

It was not appropriate to hold hands with one's assistant. It very likely... okay definitely... sent the wrong message.

"Prepare for landing," Luke said over the intercom. The words came out in a rush, sounding like one long word. An obligatory comment. One he didn't have to make at all.

Maggie and I both glanced at each other and released our hands at the same time.

"I didn't mean—" I started to apologize.

"Please," she said, shaking her head, but not looking at me. "Don't."

Where was that megawatt smile? That soft smile? Even that tolerant smile?

She was looking out the window. Not smiling at all.

Now the whole weekend was going to doubtless be awkward.

The clunk of the wheels going down was followed by the sounds of all the drop-down monitors automatically sliding back up into their places in the ceiling.

I had to get myself together. To go into work mode. To prepare to see my family.

The thought stopped me cold.

Noah had reserved rooms for us at the Whiskey Springs Saloon, which was actually a hotel crossed with a bed and breakfast with lots of history, but I had been thinking I might stay with my parents. They would expect it and besides, they had a big house that would be more comfortable than staying in a room at the old saloon.

I hadn't decided yet.

I suppose that bringing Maggie along had sort of made that decision for me. Unless I was prepared to tell her all about my personal life, we would both be staying at the Whiskey Springs Saloon Hotel.

At the push of a button, her chair went back over to her side of the aisle. I took a moment to admire the engineering that allowed seats to slide into the aisle and back with a simple push of a button.

She packed her book into her oversized leather handbag and straightened in her seat.

It occurred to me as the plane went in for a landing, that Maggie looked like she belonged on this airplane.

She did not look like an assistant who, according to her resume, had only worked for a company that only did local jobs. So that ruled out traveling with a former billionaire boss.

Even having a brother who was a pilot couldn't give her that look.

She didn't move a muscle as the wheels touched down smoothly on the little runway.

I was here to check out the terminal for Noah, but I couldn't take my eyes off Maggie.

This girl was confident, sophisticated, and beautiful as hell. She had a serene kind of beautiful. A Jackie Kennedy kind of poise.

Then she felt me staring at her and turned to face me, that megawatt smile back in place.

"Not so bad, huh?" she asked.

"No," I said, keeping my eyes on hers. "Not so bad at all."

I had a weird feeling in the pit of my stomach that I was going to be breaking my rules with this girl.

It was going to be next to impossible to keep myself in check with her.

If I had to make a guess, I'd say that having a personal relationship with an assistant was the kind of thing that Noah Worthington would never allow to happen in his world.

I took a deep breath and pulled my eyes away from hers.

Work. Work was the thing that was going to save me from what was quickly becoming a slippery slope. With every touch… every glance… I was losing my grip.

My heart would just have to figure out what to do on its own. My heart was the one having this improper attachment. So it would have to deal with it.

My head had way better sense than to think of Maggie as anything other than my well-qualified... perhaps over-qualified executive assistant.

16

MAKENNA

The wheels of the Phenom touched down in a smooth landing, just as expected.

The Whiskey Springs runway was a bit short, but Luke navigated it smoothly, then taxied *away* from what was going to be a terminal.

Couldn't have the Phenom parked anywhere near a construction site.

And that was exactly what the terminal was right now. The bones of a building. Its progress was coming right along behind the Worthington Enterprises building in Houston.

If a person didn't know better, they would think that Noah had taken a wild hair and just started constructing new buildings. I happened to know that this project in Whiskey Springs had been going on for at least a year, delayed by bad weather and about to be delayed by even more bad weather as winter set in.

What I didn't know was why it didn't get built last summer, but it wasn't my business to know so I didn't worry about it.

The Worthington Enterprises mid-rise office building in

Houston had been in various stages of production for about ten years. It had not been a wild hair by any means.

So that was that.

My heart was pounding dangerously and I could still feel Charlie's hand on mine.

My hands trembled as I gathered up my book and my water bottle and prepared to get off the plane.

I happened to know that Luke was taking the plane back to Houston after he dropped Charlie and me off. He'd probably take a break and grab some lunch first.

The thought of being stuck here without transportation was oddly disconcerting.

I could find my way back to Houston, of course. I could rent a car, hop a plane, or call Grandpa to send a plane for me. Still. It had me feeling slightly off kilter.

But mostly I was unsettled, to say the least, after spending what was only a few minutes, but seemed like forever, holding Charlie's hand.

It had been so unexpected. It had caught me completely off guard.

I should have pulled my hand away. I'd actually tried loosening my fingers a couple of times, but he was holding my hand so tightly, I don't think he even noticed.

We were here now, so I had to go back into my role as Maggie Gray. Not that I had ever left it, but still...

Although... exactly what that role was, I wasn't so sure I knew right at this particular moment.

I had come on this trip with Charlie Alexander to serve as his executive assistant. That meant I was supposed to help him keep up with his schedule and whatever else he decided I needed to do. Scheduling. Correspondence.

If I were in his shoes, I wasn't sure what I would do with an executive assistant. I liked to be hands-on with those kinds of things. Having an assistant was probably one of those things a person would become accustomed to.

Charlie had not given me any information about his schedule just yet, so I wasn't going to be of any help in that area.

I had, however, helped him, I thought with a little smile to myself. I had helped him get through his fear of flying. To be fair, not flying so much. Flying in a small jet with unexpected turbulence. Even I had been caught off guard by the air pocket that made the plane seem to drop out from under us

And I came from a long line of dedicated and experienced pilots.

Luke opened the cabin door, pushing a button and quietly lowering the steps to the ground.

The sounds of metal against metal at the construction site filled the air even before the cool mountain air flowed into the cabin, bringing a chill with it. From the smell of fir trees fresh with dewy moisture and the musty scent of wet earth, I knew it had just rained.

I was reminded just how different air in the higher elevations felt than the air in Houston. The air was drier and lighter. Fresher.

I could be born and raised in Houston, Texas and still appreciate the fresh scent following a mountain rain shower.

"We're here," I said, pulling on my wool coat and shouldering my handbag.

"So it seems," Charlie said. There was something unreadable in his expression.

With a sweep of his hand, he indicated that I should disembark before him.

"Thanks, Luke," I said as I reached the door.

With a quick glance back at Charlie and a mischievous glint in his eyes, Luke grinned. "You are welcome Maggie Gray," he said.

I narrowed my eyes at him, but he just tipped his pilot's cap. Grandpa insisted that all his pilots wear caps. Mostly the pilots complained that it made them look old-fashioned, but I thought it was rather charming.

Rolling my eyes at him, I carefully made my way down the steps.

When I reached the ground, I stepped aside and waited for Charlie.

The terminal was about the size of the Skye Travels building at the Houston airport, except that it was only one story.

And, of course, instead of being north of one of the largest cities in the country, it was in one of the most beautiful places in the country.

Whiskey Springs was nestled in a high elevation valley, deep in the heart of the Rocky Mountains. Even though we were in high elevation, even higher, rugged snowcapped mountain peaks surrounded us on all sides.

On the west side, the mountain peaks were hidden beneath clusters of white clouds. It was snowing up in the high country, I mused. As it should be, being as it was December and almost Christmas at that.

It looked like it must have just stopped raining even though the ground was barely damp. Typical mountain shower. Happened every day.

There were a few men in yellow hardhats walking about the construction site.

"You know the pilot?" Charlie asked as he reached my side.

Nothing got past Charlie Alexander.

"A little," I said. "He knows my brother."

It wasn't a lie. Of course he knew my brother. Luke and I were cousins. But it wasn't time to tell him that.

This little farce was so going to come back and bite me in the butt.

Once again, I knew... I just knew... that the longer I went without telling Charlie the truth, the worse this was going to end.

Maybe now was about as good a time as any to tell him the truth. He could go on and enjoy his time in Whiskey Springs and I could do the same. Separately.

"Looks like our car's here," he said as a white Mercedes sedan slowly made its way toward us.

I was inclined to agree with him. Since the flight was right on time, this was undoubtedly our car.

When the Mercedes stopped right next to the airplane, Luke began the transfer of our luggage from the plane to the car.

It was too late to tell Charlie now.

I smiled at the driver, whom I happily did not know as he opened the back door for me.

The driver, wearing dark sunglasses, closed my door before he went around the car to open the door for Charlie.

They spoke for a few minutes before Charlie slid inside the other door and sat next to me. I hadn't been able to understand what they said to each other, but it sounded like they might know each other.

"Do you know the driver?" I asked, with a little playful smile.

"A little," he said, with an equally amused grin.

Well. This was going to be entertaining if nothing else.

However. This was the last time I was going to let Betty get me into something like this.

I'd make sure of that.

17

CHARLIE

The air here in Whiskey Springs was crisp and clean and smelled like a Christmas tree lot.

The air hitting me in the face when I stepped off the airplane felt like a blow to the gut. When had I started to miss this place? I hadn't seen that realization coming.

I was still reeling with the unexpected pangs of bittersweetness that came with being back in Whiskey Springs when the driver came around to open the door.

"Charlie?" the driver said. "Charlie Alexander. As I live and breathe."

I lowered my sunglasses and looked at the driver. "Um..." I should know this guy... Stocky. Middle-aged. But my brain stripped out on it.

"It's me. Benjamin."

No way. "Benjamin Forester?"

"Holy shit," he said. "It is you. I didn't know if you were still living or not."

"Oh," I said. "I think you would have heard if I wasn't."

Benjamin lowered his voice. "They said I'm taking you to the saloon?" he asked with a quick glance at the car where

Maggie sat. "Do your parents know you're here?"

And just like that I remembered what I did not like about small towns. Everybody knew everything about everybody.

"Haven't told them yet," I said with a little shrug.

"Well," Benjamin said. "Your secret is safe with me."

I wasn't sure that it was a secret exactly. I hadn't gotten that far. And I knew that no matter what anyone said about secrets, there was no such thing as a secret in a small town.

Noah hadn't exactly given me enough time to think through all the implications of being back here.

I was just here to consult on the terminal he was building. And in all truthfulness, I could do that in about less than a couple of hours and be on my way back to Houston.

But apparently I was supposed to take my time. Take a couple of days. Essentially a weekend, although it was in the middle of the week.

Noah probably thought he was doing me a favor. After all, Whiskey Springs was a tourist destination. That was the whole reason Noah was building the terminal here as a matter of fact.

I settled into the backseat of the white Mercedes with black leather interior and tried to ignore the fact that Maggie was sitting merely inches away from me. Like the airplane, the car had that new car smell and yet I could still smell her cinnamony peppermint.

I had not accounted for running into anyone that I knew from here. And I had barely even stepped off the airplane.

But I knew the driver. Benjamin Forester.

Good God. He and I had gone to high school together.

Benjamin looked way more than just twelve years older than when I had last seen him.

I ran a hand along my chin and looked at the back of his head. The man had gray hair, for God's sake.

Had I aged that much?

No. I was encouraged that I hadn't recognized him until he told me who he was, but he had recognized me.

No, I decided. He had aged more than I had.

As he turned on the motor, the end of the radio announcer's message came through the speakers.

"... so expect some cold weather folks. Bundle up and stay inside. After all, 'tis the season. Ho. Ho. Ho."

Shaking my head just a little, out of embarrassment or something akin to it, I caught Maggie looking at me curiously out of the corner of her eye.

She'd been doing that a lot.

"I feel like there's something you aren't telling me," she said, leaning in my direction and keeping her voice low, after I admitted to knowing Benjamin.

I grinned. "Anybody ever tell you just how astute you are?"

She leaned close enough for me to once again catch the faint scent of wildflowers I had noticed yesterday when we had crashed into each other.

She had the most beautiful large green eyes. With her this close, the sun shining through the sunroof, the smile on her face, I could see the different shades of green, dark and light, shooting out from her pupils.

"People tell me that all the time," she said.

Looking into her eyes, I struggled to remember just what exactly I had just asked her.

I wasn't so sure it really mattered so much anyway.

What mattered right now was just how much trouble I was in.

18

MAKENNA

The radio announcer predicted cold weather. Imagine that. We were in the mountains of Colorado. I would expect no less. I pulled my woolen scarf out of my handbag and wrapped it around my neck. Then pulled out my gloves and laid them in my lap. It was plenty warm in the car, so I didn't need them until I got out.

While I was rummaging in my handbag, I pulled out my sunglasses and put them on.

I was one of the few, maybe the only person, I knew who didn't like wearing sunglasses. I liked taking in bright sunlight.

But with the roof open and the mid-day sun coming through, even I had to do something to protect my eyes.

Besides, and maybe more truthfully, it was more than a little bit disconcerting that Charlie could see my eyes, but I couldn't see his behind his sunglasses.

After slipping on my sunglasses, I looked over at him, feeling a bit smug, but he was looking out the window.

And even with dark glasses covering his eyes, I could see that his expression was... troubled.

I wanted to ask what was troubling him, but the more I

asked him, the more he was going to want to ask me and that just meant that he would find out who I was all that much sooner. Not necessarily a bad thing, I guess.

Just a few minutes ago, I had been going to tell him who I really was.

But when it came right down to it, I couldn't do it.

I had the sense that the minute I told him who I really was, he was going to send me packing, so to speak.

And right now, God help me, I was enjoying his company.

Sort of. Actually he wasn't all that personable. Rather unfriendly, all in all.

A bit confused by my own reaction, I stole a glance in his direction.

There was something about his sparkling deep blue eyes and that smile, when he dared share it, that had my heart pumping faster than was probably healthy.

And then there was the way he smelled. Earthy and smoky like a blue spruce in the rain.

Besides, I had come this far.

Betty had five daughters and eleven grandchildren. The woman had been around to know a thing or two.

Not that I was looking for someone to date. I decidedly wasn't. And I shut that train of thought down before it even got traction.

In the past two years I had gone on a couple of meaningless dates. Now that I thought about it, they had both been from well-meaning friends setting me up.

There was the guy who was so incredibly pale, I couldn't bear to look at him. The guy really needed to talk a walk in the sunlight. And on top of that, he'd made up for the lack of color in his skin by the colorful profanity that spilled from his lips every other sentence. And since he talked so much I barely got a word in edgewise, that was a lot of colorful language. I shuddered at the memory I had mostly buried into the deep discarded files of my brain where it belonged.

The other guy hadn't been much better. Self-absorbed and lived with his mother.

Such experiences did not encourage dating of random strangers.

It hurt my heart to think that when Charlie discovered who I really was, he would never speak to me again. I tried to put myself in his shoes. To think how I would feel if he was pretending to be someone else. But I couldn't do it.

It was unfathomable.

We rode in the relative silence broken only by the country music on the radio station for the fifteen minutes or so that it took to get downtown Whiskey Springs.

The driver parked parallel on the side of the two-lane street, got out, and opened my door.

Festive Christmas music immediately replaced the country music from the radio, spinning me into a nostalgic mood.

I'd been to Whiskey Springs last summer to visit my brother who had moved here to be with his fiancé.

At that time, I had dubbed it a charming, quaint little town with quite a few tourists.

It was still charming and quaint and still had a lot of tourists. But it was different. It was different because Christmas was less than a week away.

Everything was draped with garland or lights or garland and lights. I could only imagine how festive it would look at night.

I glanced at my watch. It would be a few hours yet. Right now it was lunch time and my stomach grumbled on cue.

Charlie opened his own door and together he and the driver began unloading our luggage from the trunk. His one suitcase and my two. Oddly enough, maybe not odd, both of my suitcases were larger than his. Winter, I reminded myself. Sweaters and coats were bulky.

"I'll take yours inside, Miss," the driver said, kindly.

I looked at the hotel sign. *The Whisky Springs Hotel Saloon.*

"We're staying in a saloon?" I asked, mostly to myself, but apparently out loud.

"Second most nicest hotel in town," the driver, Benjamin, said.

I nodded. I knew what the nicest place was. The Daniels House, an exclusive bed and breakfast even higher up in elevation than Whiskey Springs.

And it just so happened to belong to my brother's fiancé, her people at any rate.

As soon as we got inside, I would text my brother. See if we could get together.

Then I heard Charlie laugh and was reminded that I was here to work, not here to visit my brother. Besides, I would see him in Houston for Christmas, even though I was pretty sure he would be back here Christmas Eve. His fiancé, being from here, still had family and traditions that my brother would share with her, as he should.

That left me a small window to see my brother. Maybe I would just see him after Christmas. I took a deep breath. It would be ill-bred of me to just show up unannounced, so, I decided, maybe it was best if I flew under the radar, did my work, and went home.

Besides, as much as I hated to admit it, I had a really sneaky feeling that he and I were going to miss each other. He was probably on his way to Houston now.

As we stepped inside the saloon, the music changed from festive on the sidewalks to more classic inside the saloon.

I removed my sunglasses and waited for my eyes to adjust to the dimmer light.

It was like a regular bar. Sort of. A bar crossed with a

restaurant. In fact, instead of the usual darkness, the whole front wall was floor to ceiling glass, revealing a beautiful view of the tall rugged snow-capped mountains in the distance.

I quickly identified the source of the music. A pretty young lady dressed in a long red dress reminiscent of the late 1800s, sat playing a grand piano, her fingers moving effortlessly over the keys.

Another one of my regrets. I'd had every opportunity as a child to learn music, but I'd been more interested in the sciences. Even in grade school, I'd preferred to do extra math problems to practicing what to me had been the boring piano. No matter how long I practiced, there was never a definitive end point. With math problems, I could get to the answer and have closure. Not that I understood that at age ten.

I waited while Charlie walked up to the bar, assuming that was where we had to check in.

The huge wooden bar, something like hickory maybe, was clean and smooth. It would, probably, be made from wood readily available in this area, but I had no clue what that might be.

There was a large mirror on the wall behind the bar reflecting the street behind me, making the whole room seem at least twice as big.

I glanced at my watch again.

A place this size should have a least a dozen customers having lunch about this time. But there were all of none. There were three men sitting at a table toward the back, but they were all drinking beer from bottles.

I stole a peak at one of the menus stacked at the hostess stand. They definitely sold food. There was even a list of lunch items on the back of the one page menu.

Something seemed... off.

Then I caught part of the conversation between Charlie and the gruff sounding bar tender.

"We're closed," I heard him say.

Closed? Surely I heard wrong.

I took two steps forward so I could hear more of the conversation over the piano music that I had been enjoying until now. Now it was just annoying.

"The Daniels House?" Charlie asked.

"Roads are closed."

Then the piano player didn't want me to hear anything else. The music got louder. Either that or the men were talking in more hushed tones.

I was about to walk up to the bar to find out for myself when Charlie turned around.

"There was a water leak," he said to me. "They're closed."

Closed. So I did hear right. Didn't look like they were closed closed since there were men drinking beer at one of the tables.

"We'll just stay somewhere else."

"It's Christmas," Charlie said. "There are no more rooms in town.

19

CHARLIE

A young lady sat at the piano playing traditional Christmas music. As was typical for the historical saloon, she was wearing a vintage burlesque dress. Going with the season, her dress was candle apple red with lots of white petticoats showing beneath. Her hair was curled and secured loosely on top of her head.

I didn't recognize her and hadn't expected to. She would have been a kid when I left here ten years ago.

I had not taken the weather into account. I suppose I had lived in Houston too long where the weather was mostly hot, but heat didn't close down roads.

There was a storm coming in... one I had not bothered to know about... and it affected everything.

The storm and Christmas mixed with an unexpected water leak at the saloon, closed the whole place down, putting guests out.

The trickle down effect was simple. There were no rooms available in town.

None.

Benjamin looked over at me. "The house?" he asked.

I nodded and we wheeled our luggage toward the door. Maggie followed, a look of consternation on her face. She wasn't saying anything, but she had her cell phone out.

She looked like she was trying to figure out what we should do.

By "the house," Benjamin meant my parents' house.

Maggie's silence lasted until we stepped outside onto the sidewalk.

"What are we going to do?" she asked, her fingers hovering over the keys. I was curious what she had in mind to do about this particular situation. As my assistant, it was, after all, part of her job description to solve problems like this.

Fortunately, I did not need her to solve this one.

It was a no brainer.

Benjamin took my suitcase from my hands and wheeled it over to the trunk. He was staying out of this conversation. Smart man.

"We have to stay somewhere else," I said.

"You just said—."

"I said there were no rooms in town." There was an edge to my voice that I didn't like.

She slid her hands into her pockets and shivered as the wind blew a lock of hair across her face.

It wasn't her fault I was on edge because I was about to show up at my parents' house unexpectedly. Parents I had not visited for ten years.

And not only was I showing up, I was bringing a guest.

I already knew the conclusion they would jump to.

They would not be able to help themselves.

Before we stepped out of the car, Maggie would be my girlfriend.

I needed to warn her.

But first I needed to tell her.

Taking a deep breath, I looked steadily into her eyes. "There are no rooms available, but we can stay with my parents."

"Your...?" Sweeping her hair out of her face, she cut herself off, obviously deciding not to say whatever she had been about to.

Rubbing a hand through my hair, I looked away for a moment. It just had to be done.

"I'm from Whiskey Springs," I said.

She studied me, her eyes searching mine, for what I didn't know.

"No one told me that," she said finally.

"No one told you because no one knew."

She nodded slowly. "You didn't want Gr—anyone to know."

"It didn't seem relevant."

As we stepped aside to let a couple walk past us, the music spilling out of the sidewalk speakers changed to a lighthearted song about cold weather at Christmastime.

"But it came in handy after all," she said.

Benjamin opened the back door and she got inside the car.

I stood a moment, watching as Benjamin closed her door.

He clapped me on the shoulder. "I'd say that went pretty good."

I just nodded. I had to agree. It had gone surprisingly well.

It was interesting how Benjamin already thought she was my girlfriend. Funny how people were so quick to make assumptions.

I couldn't say that I had ever worked with a woman... and never dated one... who possessed such composure and poise.

Impressive, all in all.

Benjamin held my door open and I slid in next to Maggie. She was looking out the window, her expression blank.

"You're about to meet the parents," I said, attempting a joke.

Maggie's green eyes widened as she glanced at me then looked away again.

Benjamin got into the driver's seat and we took off down Main Street toward... home.

It was only about a five minute drive so there was no time to have a conversation.

I reminded myself that Maggie was my assistant. It wasn't natural for me to be nervous about taking her home.

Except... I couldn't stop thinking about her.

I couldn't stop thinking about the way her hair looked delightfully windswept. I couldn't stop thinking about her big beautiful bright green eyes and the way they seemed to see into my very soul.

Then there were her lips. When she wasn't smiling, like right now, they were perfectly bow-shaped. But when she smiled, her face lit up brightening not only her whole countenance, but everything around her. Her smile made the air around her hum with a glistening magic.

How was I supposed to get my mind off of her as a beautiful woman and introduce her as merely my assistant?

My parents would see right through me.

They were going to know that even if there wasn't something more going on between us, then I, at least, wanted there to be.

I leaned back against the heated leather seat and forced myself to take deep breaths.

I just needed to think. That was all. To just think.

20

MAKENNA

*I*t took less than five minutes to get from the saloon to Charlie's parents' house.

I kept my head turned toward the window for the short duration of the drive.

I needed to think.

If Charlie had been joking when he said we were going to meet the parents. He picked a funny time to make a joke.

What he didn't know was that it felt uncomfortably real to me.

First of all, what he didn't know was that I really wasn't his assistant. That was a big one.

The second thing was that I couldn't stop thinking about his sparkling blue eyes that seemed to watch me with amusement. If I didn't know better, I would have bet that he already knew I wasn't really his assistant.

I hadn't been able to stop thinking about him since we'd crashed into each other at the construction site. About how I fit perfectly against him.

Then he'd gone and held my hand on the plane. That had

sent my blood pumping crazily through my veins. I wonder if he'd been able to feel my pulse pounding against his own skin.

Knowing that I was posing as his assistant was one thing, but extending that ruse to his parents seemed like another thing entirely.

It seemed like too much.

When they found out the truth, they would ask for an explanation. A motivation. I didn't have one. Nothing more than my Grandfather's assistant, Betty, had all but challenged me to do something out of my comfort zone.

I should just tell him.

I should tell him before this went too far. Before he lied to his parents.

Was he telling a lie if he didn't know it was a lie?

I turned and looked into his dazzling blue eyes.

There was no reason not to just tell him now. Before he lied to his parents, for God's sake.

"I—"

"We're here," Benjamin announced as the car came to a stop.

I turned back to the window.

The house was bigger than anything I expected to see in Whiskey Springs, other than the Daniels House, of course. The Daniels House Hotel, built in the late 1800s, deep in the mountains was more of a castle than just a house, so it didn't count.

This house also looked like it could have been built in the 1800s. It was a large two-story white wooden house with a wraparound porch. On one side of the porch was a swing. On the other side were two wooden rocking chairs, also painted in white.

The front lawn was well-manicured for winter. A cluster of silver barked aspen trees, their leaves shed weeks ago mixed with half a dozen lovely blue spruce trees that looked like natural undecorated Christmas trees.

There was a festive wreath on the door and the six front columns were circled with wide red ribbons, flowing into big bows tied at regular intervals along the porch banister.

The big front picture window hinted of a Christmas tree with twinkling clear lights reflecting off the glass.

Altogether it kind of made the house look like one big present.

It was hard for me to imagine that Charlie had grown up here.

He seemed like such a city boy. I never would have expected him to be from here. Denver maybe. But not here.

Whiskey Springs seemed like such a quiet, peaceful place to live. Yet somehow Charlie, an urban, modern man had sprung from here.

Benjamin opened the door and I dragged myself back out into the cold and windy, but sunny day.

I waited as Charlie and Benjamin again dragged our luggage from the trunk.

I kept my hands in my pockets, not just to keep them warm, but to also keep them from trembling.

It was evident to me that Charlie was not particularly happy about coming here. The fact that he had been going to stay at the saloon hotel supported that hunch. And yet I had no idea whatsoever what the implications of all that was.

21

CHARLIE

The house was the same yet different.

My parents had bought a new sofa and two matching leather recliners.

But they had the same stockings hanging over the stone hearth fireplace.

Mom. Dad. Charlie. Bella.

The embroidered names were a little faded with time, but otherwise none the worse for wear.

The warm fire, burning real wood, crackled. I couldn't remember the last time I'd seen real wood burning. My place in Houston, like most, had gas flames.

Seeing the red stockings hanging there just like they had since I was a child, brought a lump to my throat. We'd had them so long I couldn't remember a Christmas without them.

It was my mother who hung the stockings every year in hopes that her adult children would return home for the holidays.

The guilt from knowing that was pretty much overwhelming.

So I told myself she did it out of nostalgia, not hope.

We sat in the kitchen, which hadn't changed much either except for the new refrigerator. The breakfast table with four chairs that we had used every day was the same. There were new festively red seat cushions, though, and decorative dish towels that had never been used folded neatly on the counter.

Momma used an electric pitcher to heat water for hot tea. Then she began the task of making grilled cheese sandwiches.

Daddy wasn't home. Small town doctors never really retired. They just made house calls to friends.

"I'm so glad you're here," Momma said as she slathered butter on half a dozen slices of bread before slapping them on a griddle. Honestly you'd think she was cooking for teenagers, not two adults who obviously ate very little.

I could feel Maggie looking at me, but I purposely avoided meeting her gaze.

"You should talk him into staying for the Christmas festival," she said to Maggie, not even waiting for me to answer.

"That would be nice," Maggie said.

Momma grinned and turned her back to us as she added cheese on top of the bread.

I gave Maggie a questioning look. She just shrugged and mouthed "What?"

She was right, of course. There wasn't much she could say.

I'd introduced her as my assistant.

Momma had just grinned and hugged her.

Maggie hadn't batted an eye. She had hugged Momma back and complimented her on her Christmas decorations.

They had hit it off instantly.

"So are you from Houston?" Momma asked her, over her shoulder.

"Yes," Maggie said. "Born and bred."

Momma laughed and flipped the grilled cheese. "Charlie,"

she said. "Would you look in the pantry and grab a bag of chips. Just pick whichever one you like."

I got up and went to the walk-in pantry, managing to keep my grumblings to myself.

Somehow I had imagined how much my mother had missed me. I thought she would be ecstatic to see me. I had not expected her to send me on errands while she chatted with Maggie.

You'd think Maggie was my girlfriend… or more… the way she was acting.

Their laughter spilled from the kitchen. I just rolled my eyes and pulled a bag of barbeque chips off one of the shelves.

I never would have imagined that she would practically ignore me and take to Maggie like they were long lost friends.

She did understand that Maggie was my assistant, right? I don't think she would have been more taken with her if I'd introduced her as my girlfriend.

I had never brought a girlfriend home.

Hell, I hadn't even brought myself home for ten years.

I went back in the kitchen and sat back down.

They were talking about the Galleria in Houston.

As far as I knew, my mother had never even been to Houston. I know she'd never come to visit me. They were talking about it, but the timing had never worked out right.

"My younger cousin ice skates," Maggie said. "She's seven years old, but already they think she'll go to the Olympics."

I just stared at Maggie as she spoke. My mother knew more about her in thirty minutes than I knew and I had been the one to hire her.

I ripped the chips open, grabbed a handful to munch on, and leaned back in my chair.

It didn't matter so much to me that Maggie had an Olympic bound seven-year-old niece.

What mattered to me was the way she looked into my soul with her stunningly clear green eyes. And those red lips. Those red kissable lips that would send a man to his knees. This man anyway.

22

MAKENNA

The Alexander's kitchen was charmingly homey. I'd been right about it being built in the 1800s, but it didn't seem that old. It had been well taken care of over the centuries.

The kitchen, in fact, was as modern as my condo in Houston. Recently painted in a nice cream color, it was clean. About half the top cabinets had glass doors and the glasses and plates behind it were all neatly and spaciously arranged.

A pan of fresh muffins on one end of the cabinet scented up the house. If she offered one of those, there was no way I was going to be able to refuse.

Mrs. Alexander made THE best grilled cheese that I had ever eaten. Either that or it was elevation induced appetite.

But I was betting on it being the first. It had lots of gooey cheese and fresh tomato right in the middle.

I had a weakness for potato chips, so the grilled cheese with chips was mouth-wateringly delicious and I ate the whole thing.

"Would you like another one?" Mrs. Alexander asked as she placed a second sandwich on Charlie's plate.

He was shaking his head and pushing at the plate, but she ignored him.

Finally, with a roll of his eyes, he gave in and ate it anyway.

"I couldn't possibly," I said. "But thank you. It was wonderful."

"I like to see a girl with an appetite," Mrs. Alexander said. "Girls these days are too skinny."

I laughed.

Charlie groaned. "Maggie," he said. "Please take that as a compliment."

"It's okay," I said. "She's right. And I do." As a perfect size six, I was healthy and didn't take offense to any reference about my weight, one way or the other.

I grabbed some more chips just to prove that I wasn't the least bit offended.

"Charlie," she said. "I have a couple of things ordered at the General Store that someone needs to pick. Why don't you and Maggie take a walk down there and pick them up? Show her downtown."

"We just came from downtown," he grumbled as he finished his second sandwich.

It was cute, really, how such a successful businessman caved beneath his mother's insistence.

His mother was painfully transparent. Charlie had introduced me as his assistant, but I could see that she didn't believe that for a minute.

I was grateful that she didn't ask me anything about work. Charlie had told her that I didn't start work until January.

She had lifted an eyebrow at that and taken her assumptions from there. I chose not to think about it, since I was the one pretending to be Maggie.

And so far I had not lied about anything other than my name.

Mrs. Alexander had already figured out that Charlie and I barely knew each other.

"But before you go, you have to try one of my muffins. If they turn out, I'm going to take them to the Festival of Trees."

I glanced over at Charlie. There was a whole lot being thrown at us. He was watching me, his eyes hooded, his expression blank. I would give anything to know what he was thinking right about now.

"What's the Festival of Trees?" I asked.

"It's the first of three days of Christmas celebrations in town. It ends with a Christmas dance on Christmas Eve," she said, pulling the tray of muffins over and arranging them on a plate.

"It starts tomorrow?" I asked, calculating the time in my head.

"That's right," Mrs. Alexander said with a pleased grin.

"I thought it was a Christmas supper," Charlie said, not breaking a smile.

"It is," Mrs. Alexander said as she placed two muffins on different plates and set them in front of us before she slid into a chair across from us. "It's both."

She clasped her hands in front of her and waited, looking expectantly from one of us to the other.

"Aren't you going to have one?" I asked, toying with the paper on the outside of the muffin.

"She's going to let us try them first," Charlie said. "See if they're any good."

Mrs. Alexander grinned. "He knows me so well."

"Well," I said. "You don't have to ask me twice." With a grin, I peeled the paper off the muffin and took a bite.

I closed my eyes as I chewed.

"This is sooo good," I said, opening my eyes and looking at Charlie.

My breath hitched as I caught the expression on his face.

He was watching me with an intensity in his sparkling blue eyes and a little half grin on his face.

I swallowed thickly, well aware that his mother was sitting across from us.

But no matter.

I was in trouble.

This could definitely be a problem.

Then I remembered that he thought I was someone else entirely.

It was a good thing I wasn't really his assistant.

That could really be a whole host of other problems.

Right now my main problem was having him not find out who I was.

At least if I wanted to stay.

And I wanted to stay.

23

CHARLIE

How was it that a grown man was always a boy in the presence of his mother?

Less than one hour after we finished lunch, Maggie and I were bundled up again and heading outside to make the walk to Main Street.

The sun was still out, warm on the top of my head, but the wind was cold. The mix of hot and cold was intriguing.

The clouds that had been clustered around the tops of the rugged mountains were drifting away from the peaks, coming this way. It was going to be snowing before long.

I'd taken a minute to check the weather on my phone while Maggie was freshening up in the guest room.

There was snow coming in. And not just a little bit. If it snowed the way they were predicting, there was no way we were going to be getting out of here after today.

Downtown wasn't far. Using the cut off, we could be on Main Street in ten minutes.

Following the road, it would be twenty, depending on how fast we walked.

I was inclined to follow the road.

Despite my reluctance to get too involved, I wanted Maggie to see everything.

I'd seen a different side of her when she'd been talking to my mother. A playful side I hadn't expected. And friendly. She was exceptionally likeable. Of course, I'd only known her for a little over twenty-four hours.

It seemed like longer.

We walked past the fragrant blue spruce trees, quickly reaching the sidewalk.

"It smells like Christmas," Maggie said. "I mean, I know it IS Christmas, but it actually smells like it."

"It's the trees," I said.

She grinned, looking up at me sideways. "It's nice."

We headed toward town and within a few minutes I could hear the Christmas music spilling out from the speakers downtown.

"Do you miss it here?" she asked.

"Maybe. Sometimes." I stuck my hands in my pockets to keep from reaching for her hand. "I mostly miss it when I'm here. Does that make sense?"

"Oddly enough, it does," she said. "When you're not here, you don't think about it."

"No." I waved at two little girls and a little boy playing in the yard as we passed what used to be old Mr. Johnson's house. There was a brightly painted swing out front and toys scattered everywhere. Apparently old Mr. Johnson didn't live there anymore.

"How long has it been?" Maggie asked. "Since you were here?"

"Ten years." There was no point in not telling her. Not now. She was going to be spending the night at my parents' house and from the looks of the weather, it was going to be more than a night or two.

"Wow," she said. "I can't imagine not seeing my family for

ten years. It was hard going a semester at a time not seeing them when I was in college."

"You went to the University of Houston," I said. "And you didn't see them?"

She looked at little startled and missed a step.

"Look," she said. "The lights are on already."

I followed her gaze. The lights were on. All of downtown twinkled in the haze of the cloudy afternoon.

I felt a little nostalgic pang. I hadn't been lying when I'd said I missed it here when I was here.

It was much much easier to just stay away. As long as I stayed away, I didn't have to deal with missing the little town or my parents or the guilt.

Maggie was huddled in her woolen coat, her hands in her pockets, her nose a little pink.

"Do you like hot chocolate?" I asked.

"Who doesn't?" she asked with a little shrug.

"Then I have to take you to Smedley's Ice Cream Parlor. They have THE best hot chocolate anywhere."

"The best, huh?" she said. "Lead the way."

I looped an arm with hers.

She was completely adorable with her skin flushed from the cold. As her eyes met mine, looking at me from beneath her lashes, her lips curved into a most beguiling smile.

I was quickly learning that it was hard to keep my hands off of her. And from the looks of her expression, she knew it.

It was a bit humbling to know that she knew I was taken with her.

I didn't know what I was going to do about her being my assistant just yet.

That was going to require some thinking. Some thinking I hadn't had the opportunity to do yet.

There had to be a solution.

I just didn't know what it was yet.

It would be so much easier if she wasn't working for me. If she wasn't working for me, I'd just dispense with all the game playing, pull her right against me, and kiss her soundly on the lips.

24

MAKENNA

Modern pop Christmas music, my favorite, spilled from the speakers in Smedley's Ice Cream Parlor.

Charlie and I sat at one of the little tables painted in bright candle apple red on matching red wooden chairs.

There was a line of customers inside the shop and we had to stand in line a few minutes to place our order.

Charlie ordered for me, since he seemed to want me to try the hot chocolate float. Hot chocolate with ice cream.

And he had made the right choice.

We each sat with a tall glass mug in front of us, filled to the brim with a unique mixture of hot chocolate and little balls of vanilla ice cream. They actually tasted more like little balls of soft whipped cream to me.

Whatever it was, it was delightful.

"Do you like it?" Charlie asked, using his spoon to take a sip.

"I've never tasted anything like this," I said. "And I live in Houston."

"I guess sometimes we have to get out of the city to experience things you can't get there."

"Maybe," I said, looking toward the window, not really seeing the families, all bundled up, walking up and down the sidewalk.

Not really seeing the jolly Santa Clause across the street, ringing his oversized bell. People actually stopping and putting coins in his bucket instead of pretending they didn't see him.

Instead, my brain was working at high speed.

Smedley's Ice Cream Parlor.

In Houston.

It would be successful. I knew it would. I was Houston born and bred and it was the best thing I'd ever tasted as far as hot chocolate. And ice cream. Together.

We could start by opening one in Katy. One in Sugarland. Maybe the Woodlands. Get them going. Build up the reputation. Then put one in Uptown Houston. Maybe in the Galleria.

"Maggie?"

I could do it. I could make it work.

"Who's the owner?" I asked, setting down my spoon and looking over at Charlie.

"Maggie," Charlie said. "Where did you go?" He might have been trying to get my attention. I wasn't sure.

"I just had the best idea."

"What's that?" he asked, looking more than a little skeptical.

"Smedley's Ice Cream Parlor in Houston."

He was looking at me with an odd expression.

"It could work. I'm assuming this is the only one. Family owned?"

"They'd have to have an investor," he said, not answering me. "It would be a process."

"A process I could—"

Charlie reached out. Put a hand on mine.

I stopped. Took a deep breath. Cleared my throat.

A process I could make happen.

A family with two young children sat down at a table next to us. The two children had ice cream cones and chattered nonstop.

"You're right," I said, sweetly, backing off. Backing way off. "It would be a process." I took another sip of the heavenly hot chocolate. "I just wish we had one of these in Houston."

"Maybe one day," he said, with a little shrug. "You never know what could happen."

You never know indeed.

I tucked my hands inside my coat pockets and looked around. Didn't he see it? This place was crowded. Smedley's Ice Cream Parlor was a hit in Whiskey Springs. Especially with hot chocolate ice cream like this.

But I tucked my enthusiasm away for another day.

I'd almost given myself away.

I'd almost told Charlie that *I* could be the investor. *I* could make it all happen.

But it would not be in my best interest to tell him that.

At least, even if Charlie ran me out of his life after he discovered my true identity, I could come back here and talk to the owner about investing in an expansion into the Houston area. I would have gotten something more than a huge crush out of this trip.

The problem was. I would trade it all to keep things going as they were with Charlie.

To have him find out that I was in fact not his assistant and for him to feel the way I did.

25

CHARLIE

One of my favorite, albeit nostalgic, songs about making it home for Christmas spilled over the speakers in Smedley's Ice Cream Parlor.

The place smelled like chocolate and peppermint and everything decadent.

If the chair had been an inch smaller, it would have been too small for me to sit in. As it was, I felt a big like a man sitting at a child's table.

Maggie, on the other hand, looked quite comfortable sitting across from me.

There was a passion in her eyes as she talked about what was essentially franchising Smedley's Ice Cream Parlor.

She had a degree in business, but still... She couldn't possibly know just how complex such an endeavor actually was.

I found it rather cute and charming that she thought she could just have an idea like that and make it happen.

Maybe this was the kind of thing she and her previous employer had talked about.

I decided that I would find out.

"Tell me about your previous employer," I said. "I apologize, but I've forgotten his name."

Her fingers froze on her glass and she looked a bit stunned for a second.

"Is this a job interview?" she asked, adding a little laugh.

"Of course not," I said. "I've already hired you. I'm just curious what kinds of things you did." I smiled. "You might have secret talents that I need to tap into."

There was that stunned expression again, but she shrugged it off and brought her glass to her lips before she answered. "Just the usual assistant things," she said, looking out the window behind me. "Scheduling and making appointments and such."

"That's kind of the same thing," I said under my breath.

"What's that?" She looked back at me, her green eyes latching onto mine and holding.

"Scheduling," I said. "And making appointments. Kind of the same thing."

"I guess," she said, a little frown at the center of her brow. "Nuances."

She said it so softly I barely heard her.

"What kind of company was it?" I asked. I'd seen the name listed on her resume, but it hadn't rung a bell with me and I had promptly forgotten it.

"Aviation," she said, the word slipping off her lips so quickly I almost missed it.

"Avia—" Of course. It made perfect sense. That was why she was so knowledgeable about the plane we had flown in on.

"I'm sorry," she said, pulling her phone out of her handbag and frowning at it. "I need to return this call."

I was about to ask her something, but what that something was I couldn't say for the life of me.

I watched as she got up and dashed from the table.

She stepped outside onto the street, pulling her scarf

around her neck and looping it loosely. The wind tousled her hair.

She looked right, then left, and darted off to the left out of my sight.

With a sigh of frustration, I leaned back and looked at her empty chair.

It was almost like she didn't want to talk about herself.

Maybe she really had just missed a call.

Leaving our empty glasses on the table, I went to the window and looked out.

A Santa Clause stood across the street, ringing a big gold bell. It was starting to get dark, waking up the colorful twinkling Christmas lights that covered just about everything that didn't move.

I did not know what I was going to do.

What exactly was a man supposed to do when he found himself falling for his assistant? One who wasn't even officially on the payroll.

I pressed my hands against my head as I considered my options. I suppose I could not hire her. Tell her it wasn't a good fit. Tell her I wanted to date her instead. But I quickly dismissed that option.

That was insane. I couldn't take the girl's job away just because I *liked* her.

A teenage boy and girl walked past, hand in hand, smiling at each other with such hope and innocence it nearly broke my heart.

There was only one solution.

I had to stop liking her.

It was the thing to do.

The right thing to do.

The only option.

26

MAKENNA

I walked along a side street, clutching my phone in one hand.

The skies were gray, holding a clear promise of snow. Technically altostratus clouds. A person didn't hang around pilots as much as I did and not learn a bit about weather.

As I walked past two different shop doors, different Christmas songs spilled out, mixing with the music piped onto the street. It was a cacophony, but not an unpleasant one.

I hadn't really missed a call.

I had just really really needed to get away from Charlie and his questions.

He was treading uncomfortably close to learning that I wasn't who I claimed to be.

My fingers trembled as I located the copy of Maggie's resume that Betty had sent me.

But instead, I dropped my phone to my side, not opening the file. If I couldn't answer his questions without looking at someone else's background, then I didn't need to answer them.

I already felt like a fraud of the utmost caliber. Not a good thing. If one was going to be high caliber, being a fraud didn't seem like the best of choices.

I paced down the street. Walked past a crowded local burger joint called the Hungry Hat that had my stomach growling. I was a sucker for a burger and fries, especially one that wasn't fast food.

Then I turned and paced back toward Main Street. I couldn't be gone long.

Didn't want to be gone long.

Betty had gotten me into this. Betty could get me out.

Taking a deep, calming breath, I sent her a text.

ME: *Charlie is asking me questions about Maggie's job history.*

I stared at my phone. Counted to ten. Betty did not respond.

Maybe I should just call her. I glanced at my watch. She could be driving home.

Then she responded.

BETTY: *Really? I thought for sure he would have figured it out by now.*

I stared at the statement. The most unexpected of statements.

Surely Betty had not sent me off on this trip thinking that I would be found out sooner rather than later.

A fool. I felt like a fool.

Just as I slid my phone into my coat pocket, unable to look at that message for another minute, Charlie appeared at the street corner.

He stopped and just stood there looking at me. He was wearing a long black woolen coat, similar to mine, his hands in his pockets.

My heart did a funny little summersault. There was something about the way he was looking at me.

I was pretty sure this was new. It was his eyes. His eyes smiled at me. They actually smiled.

Taking a step forward, I couldn't help but smile back. I felt a little bit like the Grinch. Like my heart was growing, ready to burst with happiness.

I already liked Charlie, but I was getting the impression that he liked me too and that made me like him all the more.

We met halfway down the street.

He took my hands in his. He was wearing gloves. I wasn't.

Squeezing my hands between his, I thought he was going to ask me where my gloves were. It was what I expected him to ask.

But instead, he asked me something else.

"Want to get a hamburger?" he asked.

My stomach growled again and I glanced over my shoulder. "At the Hungry Hat?" I forced myself to keep a straight face saying the name of out loud.

"They used to be the best," he said.

"Smells like it," I said. "There's a line though."

"Always a line at the good places," he said. "I don't mind waiting. Do you?"

I shook my head.

"Not really."

In truth, I would wait anywhere with him.

Charlie Alexander was stealing my heart.

And there wasn't a thing I could do about it.

27

CHARLIE

The gray clouds promised snow on the way. Tonight, if I was a betting man.

I found myself actually looking forward to the snow. It had been ten years since I had been here and ten years since I had encountered snow, much less a white Christmas.

I'd gone from Louisiana Tech in north Louisiana to Houston. Very different weather than here where there was almost always a white Christmas.

The line to get into the Hungry Hat turned out to be longer than we expected, but we made our way through the crowds of waiting customers and got good seats at the bar while we waited for our table.

The hamburger joint was a locally owned, obviously still very popular restaurant. Although the food was all American French fries and burgers, they played Mexican music in the background while everybody else in town played Christmas music. I couldn't tell if the Mexican music was Christmassy or not. Didn't sound like it.

There was a big blue spruce up by the door, lit with sparkling clear lights. The only decorations on it were pinecones and red berries. I wondered if they were finished with it or if they had more decorating to do. Probably finished, I decided, since there were only four days until Christmas.

"Would you like a glass of wine?" I asked, speaking over the conversations swirling all around us.

"Sure," she said, shrugging out of her coat.

"I don't think there's a coat closet here," I said, looking around.

"It's okay. I'll just hold onto it."

"Can we get a bottle of Louis Rose Brut?" I asked the bartender.

"Sure," the bartender, a clean-cut guy in his thirties said.

As he walked off to get the wine, Maggie looked at me with a curious expression. "I'm surprised you can get that here," she said.

And I was surprised that she knew wine. Seemed like I was learning something new about Maggie Gray every few minutes.

"It's Whiskey Springs," I said. "You can get just about anything, especially alcohol."

"Doesn't seem like—" Her phone vibrated and she glanced at the text with a scowl.

"Anything wrong?" I asked.

"No," she said, sliding her phone into her handbag. "Not at all."

A couple of seconds later the bartender came back with a bottle of pink wine and two glasses.

We watched in companionable silence as he deftly uncorked the bottle, then poured a splash of wine into two glasses.

"You look familiar," he said, looking at me.

No sense in fighting it. "Charlie Alexander," I said.

"You don't say." The bartender's face lit up. "Your father saved my father's life a few weeks back."

I glanced over at Maggie.

"None of us thought Dad was going to make it, but Doc Alexander performed a miracle."

"Glad to hear that," I said.

"My name is Teddy," the bartender said. "This wine is on the house. Dinner too. Anything you want."

"You don't have to—"

"I insist," Teddy said. "Consider it a small token of appreciation."

"Thank you," I said.

As Teddy wiped down the bottle with a white cloth, I was reminded of one of the things I did like about small towns.

Everyone knew everyone.

And people actually seemed to care about each other.

It was, I thought, ironically, the flip side of the same coin that I didn't like about small towns.

Maggie and I lifted our glasses.

"To new beginnings," I said.

I didn't begin to know what I meant by that.

The words just sort of slipped unchecked from my lips.

Maggie looked at me curiously as she did more often than not before taking a drink.

"This is good," she said.

"I like it that it's not too heavy," I said.

She swirled the wine in her glass and sniffed it.

There.

Another gesture that told me she belonged somewhere else.

Most people just tipped up their glass and drank. Most people didn't bother to savor the scent.

Only someone who frequented nice restaurants, country clubs and exclusive social events. Or at least were around people who did.

Again, my curiosity about Maggie was piqued.

But I didn't say anything. I didn't want to frighten her away again.

Maggie, I was learning, was someone I had to tread carefully around.

I hadn't figured just why, but she was.

Taking a sip of the wine, I and mentally ran down my list of things I needed to do while I was here.

I needed to take a look at Noah's airport terminal, which was, of course, the main reason I was here. Other than that, I really didn't have much I had to do.

Pulling out my phone, I set it on the bar in front of us and opened my weather app.

She leaned forward. "What are we looking at?" she asked.

"Just checking out the weather," I said. "You know, it's quite possible that we're not going to get out of here as planned."

Looking a little alarmed, she set her glass on the bar and leaned over to look at my radar app.

"This looks bad," she said. "Really bad. Can I see?"

At my nod, she lifted my phone and studied the radar screen. Then looked back at me. "We might be stuck here for Christmas," she said.

"It's quite possible," I said.

"I 'um…" she lowered my phone and sat back, not looking at me. "I need to go to the lady's room."

She got up and disappeared into the crowd, heading to the restrooms.

And just like that, she had run off again.

Seems I had a lot to learn about Maggie Gray.

28

MAKENNA

I wove my way through the crowd, zigzagging past the tables, making my way blindly to the restroom on the other side of the restaurant.

Fajitas sizzled at someone's table and the table across from them had hot apple pie and ice cream. It was more, it seemed, than just a hamburger place. If it tasted half as good as it smelled, it could see why it was so crowded.

The Mexican music, barely audible over the swirl of conversations, turned Christmassy.

I was feeling... what I could only describe as mixed.

Being stuck here in Whiskey Springs with Charlie was most appealing. That was not a problem.

What was a problem was that I had never spent a Christmas away from my family.

I stepped into the restroom and examined my appearance in the mirror.

I took a hairbrush out of my handbag and ran it through my hair.

If I was stuck here, then I had a good excuse for not being

home. I didn't know if my brother was going to be here or in Houston. I felt completely out of the loop.

I leaned against the sink, then took out a tube of red lipstick.

This was not such a bad thing.

Being stuck here for Christmas most definitely had its appeal.

I washed my hands and headed back out.

About halfway across the restaurant on my way back to the bar, just as I saw Charlie up ahead, I heard someone call my name.

"Makenna?"

I stopped. No one was supposed to know me here.

Turning to my right, I saw someone who looked familiar.

It was Evette, one of the people I had met last summer when I'd been here to visit my brother. Evette was a middle-aged woman, friends with my soon to be sister-in-law's people. She had visited the Daniels House while I was there. Had dinner with us.

"Evette," I said, darting a quick glance toward Charlie. He did not appear to have seen me yet. He was talking to the bartender.

"It's so good to see you," she said, pulling me into a hug. "What are you doing here? I thought your brother was already on his way to Houston."

Well. Evette apparently knew more than I did. "I… 'um… work," I said. "I'm here for work."

Faux work, but work nonetheless.

"Oh," she said. "You'll have to tell me all about it. Why don't you come by the house? Looks like you're going to snowed in for a few days. Christmas probably. If you don't have anywhere to go for Christmas, you have to spend it with us."

"Thank you," I said. "That's very kind of you."

Charlie stood up, the buzzer in his hand lighting up, indicating that our table was ready.

"I'm actually having dinner with a business associate," I said, putting a hand on her arm. "I have to go."

"Of course," she said, hugging me again. "Take care of yourself."

After extricating myself from Evette, I joined Charlie at the bar.

"Ready?" he asked.

"Of course."

We settled in at our table next to the window.

Charlie clasped his hands together on the table in front of him and leaned forward, his blue eyes locked onto mine.

"How is it possible," he asked. "That you know someone in Whiskey Springs?"

"I—." Swallowing hard, I realized that he had actually seen me with Evette. It would have been hard to miss since she had hugged me twice.

It occurred to me that I was at a crossroads.

I could either weave more lies or tell him the truth.

There was, of course, a third option. I could hedge.

"It's a small world," I said with a little smile. "And Whiskey Springs is quite the destination town."

He didn't believe me. I could see it in his face.

"Uh huh," he said. "That's funny because I happen to know her. Her name is Evette and she lives here."

"Are you sure?" I said, glancing over my shoulder, pretended to look for Evette.

"I'm certain," he said. "So what are you not telling me?"

I shook my head, bit my lip, and sat back.

Before I could formulate an answer, the server stopped by to take our order.

"What would you like?" Charlie asked.

"Just a burger and fries," I said, feeling a sinking in the pit of my stomach.

"I'll have the same," he said, handing the server our menus.

After the server left, he sat back and looked at me with a little smile.

"Well," I said, trying to divert his attention away from his question about how I knew Evette. "This is most definitely a popular place."

"Always has been," he said, his sparkling blue eyes filled with a bit of amusement, locked onto mine.

"What's it like?" I asked. "Being back here after all these years."

"Not as bad as I expected," he said.

I sipped my wine a moment. "Why did you think it would be so bad?"

He sat back, shook his head, and swirled the wine in his glass. "You know. I don't really have a good answer for that. I think I just always wanted to get out of here so bad. I thought if I came back…"

"That you'd be stuck."

"How'd you know?" he asked. "You're not from a small town."

I shrugged. "I'm familiar with the concept."

He narrowed his eyes as he looked at me. Then he leaned forward again.

"So tell me again how you know Evette."

29

CHARLIE

The Hungry Hat was crowded and it was hard to hear, so I scooted my chair over closer to Maggie's.

The music had turned Christmassy and seemed to get louder in a synergistic fashion as the customer's voices increased.

Even though it was loud, I liked it. It was like being in a little bubble with Maggie.

It wasn't nice to put her on the spot like that about Evette. Even as I knew it, I did it anyway.

I couldn't help myself.

Somehow, I thought if I could get the answer to how she knew Evette, I would be able to solve the mystery of *her*.

But instead of answering my question, she turned her megawatt smile on me. "You don't get to know *everything*," she said.

I studied her perfect heart shaped face framed by loose brunette hair.

Something about those red bow-shaped lips made my heart flutter irrationally.

I wanted to understand her. I wanted to know *everything* about her, even though she seemed to think that I didn't get to.

"You could give me a little something about yourself," I said. "After all, you know pretty much everything about me know."

Biting her bottom lip, she seemed to consider this.

"Okay," she said, leaning forward. "You're right. I do know a lot about you."

I nodded once in agreement.

"I come from a large family," she said. "A close family."

"I heard you telling my mother about your cousin, the ice-skater."

"That's right," she said with a little smile.

"There's a broad range in your ages," he said. "Your cousins."

"Very much," I said. "I think it's a good thing. We can all help each other out."

"What about you?" I asked. "Do you have children?" I asked casually, but I feared the answer. As an employer, I wasn't really supposed to ask personal questions like that, but it seemed like something a man could get away with asking over a glass of wine.

She didn't wear a ring, but that didn't really mean anything these days.

Before she could answer, the server brought our food and asked if we needed anything else.

Maggie speared a French fry and seemed to have forgotten my question.

Realizing that she might be ignoring it on purpose, I decided to let it go. But then she answered me.

"I don't have any children," she said.

"Neither do I."

For some reason, that made her smile to herself.

I wanted to ask if she was in a relationship, but if I did that, it would indicate that I was interested in exploring a relationship with her.

As her employer, that was contraindicated. So I didn't say anything.

And she didn't volunteer anything.

"How did you end up in engineering when your father is a doctor?" she asked.

"I always liked fixing things. Things, not people."

She nodded. "I understand. I have a couple of aunts who are psychologists. They fix people. And my uncles are…" She glanced up at me as she took a bite out of her hamburger, using the time to stall. "more mechanically inclined."

She hadn't said anything wrong. Maybe I was just looking for something. But saying she had aunts that were psychologists was very specific. Saying that her uncles were mechanically inclined was very vague.

"Mechanically inclined," I repeated.

She shrugged and tried to pass it off with a smile.

Yes. There was most definitely something she was not telling me.

For the hundredth time, I decided that Maggie Gray was not who she seemed to be.

30

MAKENNA

We stepped out onto the sidewalk outside the Hungry Hat into not only sudden quietness, but a burst of cold wind.

A few airy snowflakes fluttered delicately from the moonlit sky.

"It's snowing," I said with a bit of awe. I stopped in the middle of the street and, looking up, turned in a complete circle.

Charlie took my arm in his, turning me back in the right direction. "It's pretty isn't it?"

"It's beautiful."

"A white Christmas is one of the things I miss most about living here."

We reached Main Street and turned left, heading back toward his parents' house.

Other than the Hungry Hat, the town was mostly closed down. Just empty shops lit by bright twinkly Christmas lights.

A couple of cars and a pickup truck, headlights bright, made their way slowly along the street.

We passed a row of blue spruce trees, limbs hanging over

the sidewalk, already collecting a coating of white snow powder. The trees seemed to smell stronger in the snowy cold. Like Christmas.

The rugged mountain peaks in the distance glowed in the moonlight. The snow clouds that had been gathered around them earlier had shifted away now, leaving them exposed, showing off a new layer of snow.

"Do you ever think about coming back here?" I asked. "I mean, not now, but later, when you're older maybe?"

"Maybe," he said. "That's the one thing I've learned. Never say never."

"That's true," I said, thinking about how I ended up here in Whiskey Springs with him.

I wasn't quite sure how I had let that happen, but I was glad I did.

There was just one problem.

Charlie suspected something. I could see it in the way he asked me about Evette.

If I'd been in his shoes, I would be suspicious, too.

It was rather odd.

But I had to give him credit. He called me on it, but he didn't push.

I'd gotten myself into something of a mess. If I told him now that I wasn't really Maggie, and he asked me to go, I had nowhere else to go.

The town had no rooms. The roads were closed due to the impending storm. I couldn't get to the Daniel's House. I couldn't get a flight out of here.

My phone chimed again and I ignored it again.

I kept my hands tucked in my coat pockets as we reached the Alexander's house. Their Christmas tree filled the front window with colorful twinkly lights.

I felt a pang of homesickness. At not being home for Christmastime.

The cold wind stung my cheeks and tousled my hair into my eyes. I swept it back and looked over at Charlie. He squeezed my arm and smiled at me, setting off a flutter of butterflies in my stomach.

I smiled back.

And that was all it took for me to be okay with being here. His smile was like a balm to my troubled soul.

Charlie Alexander might not know my real name and he might think I was his assistant, but everything else about me was real.

Including the way I was falling for him.

31

CHARLIE

"Where is everybody?" Maggie asked as we stepped into the warmth of my parents' house.

"I don't know," I said, helping her out of her coat covered with a light dusting of powered snow.

"Gone up to bed already?"

"It's still early," I said, hanging her coat in the coat closet. "Maybe they're upstairs in their sitting room."

The house smelled like a Christmas bakery. My mother had been making muffins again.

As we passed the stairway, strains of classical Christmas music drifted from upstairs, confirming my suspicions that my parents were upstairs in their sitting room, probably having a glass of wine, enjoying looking out at the snowfall through their floor to ceiling window that had a magnificent view of the Rocky Mountains.

"Feel like being bad?" I asked, shrugging out of my coat.

Maggie's eyes widened. "Bad how?"

I chuckled to myself and took her hand. "Let's grab one of Momma's muffins."

She laughed. "Oh. You are very bad."

"Are you saying you don't want one?"

Her eyes lit up with devilishness. "I never said that."

Together, we tiptoed into the kitchen and found four dozen muffins sitting on the counter to cool.

I picked up two, handed one of Maggie.

"You know," she said. "your mother probably had these counted out for a reason."

"Knowing my mother," I said. "I'm sure she did. But I also know that she will get over it."

We took our muffins and went into the living room to sit on the couch in front of the tree.

I took a few minutes to get the fire going, then sat back on my heels when I had the flames roaring jauntily over the dry wood.

"Nice fire," Maggie said, as I wiped my hands on my pants and sat next to her.

"Thanks. It's been awhile since I had the pleasure."

We both began peeling the paper from our muffins and took a bite.

"Your mother is a very bad influence," she said.

"It's a good thing we don't live here, isn't it?"

"It is," she said, without a hitch.

But my own words belatedly sank into my consciousness. I said *we*.

I barely knew Maggie and I was thinking of us as *we*.

I was typically a bit... a lot... standoffish. I didn't date casually and I didn't date much. I told myself I preferred it that way.

But with Maggie sitting next to me, the flames of the fire casting shadows over her features, the warmth of the fire seeping through my skin... I found myself thinking about how much I enjoyed having her here with me.

I even found myself thinking about how it might not be so bad visiting here as long as she was with me.

My father had yet to meet her, but my mother liked her and that went a long way.

She had a big family, so we would have to figure out how to split up the holidays. Maybe my parents could go to Houston and we could all be one big happy family.

I hadn't met her family, of course, but a family that produced someone as wonderful as Maggie had to be good people.

"What are you thinking about?" she asked, finishing off her muffin.

"Not thinking about anything. Just sitting here letting my mind go blank."

She laughed softly. "Somehow I doubt that."

"Well," I said. "It could happen."

"*Could* covers a lot of ground," she said, with a little nod.

"What are you thinking about?" I asked, changing the subject away from me.

"Just thinking about how nice this is. Sitting here in front of the fire."

"It is nice," I said, looking at her profile, feeling something I hadn't felt for a very long time tug at my heart.

I needed to bring up the whole conundrum with her being my assistant. I didn't want to, but I felt like it needed to be done.

Looking at her kissable lips and knowing she was off limits was just about to drive me crazy.

"Maggie, I—"

Her phone chimed again.

"Do you need to get that?" I asked. "Your phone has been blowing up for a while now."

"Maybe," she said, pulling her phone out of her pocket. "Probably."

She looked at the screen, then looked back at me.

"It's 'um... it's my grandfather," she said.

32

MAKENNA

*T*he flickering flames mixed with the twinkling lights on the tree. The scent of muffins filled the air, reminding me of my grandmother's house at Christmastime. When we were all together. Making cookies. Gingerbread houses. Hot chocolate.

It wasn't cold in the house, but I was drawn to the warmth of the fire.

Red Christmas stockings hung from the mantel.

Mom. Dad. Charlie. Bella.

Bella, I presumed, was Charlie's sister. No one had mentioned her, so I could only wonder.

Right now, all I could do was stare at my phone. At the texts I had been ignoring.

GRANDPA: *On my way to Whiskey Springs*

GRANDPA: *Betty told me you need a flight out*

GRANDPA: *Where are you staying? The Whiskey Springs Saloon is closed.*

GRANDPA: *Need to get out before the weather turns bad*

Still holding my phone in my hands, I looked over at Charlie.

"Everything okay?" he asked.

I glanced back at the string of unanswered text messages. "I don't really know."

The thing I mostly didn't know about was Charlie.

Had Betty told Grandpa about my ruse?

Surely she had.

I couldn't imagine Betty keeping a secret like that to herself for very long. She'd admitted that she didn't think I would have been able to keep it up.

No. She hadn't told Grandpa Noah. I didn't know how I knew it, I just knew it.

But there was something strange going on.

It looked like it was time to come clean, whether I liked it or not.

"Anything I can do to help?" Charlie asked.

"I don't think so," I said.

When the doorbell rang, neither one of us moved.

I was about to ask Charlie if he was going to answer it, when we heard footsteps coming down the stairs.

"Come in," Charlie's father, Doc Alexander said. "Good to see you."

"I appreciate you letting me stay here for the night." My grandfather's voice sent all sorts of emotions through me.

One of them, in this particular moment, was to hide. I felt like a kid who had done something wrong.

I sat up straight on the couch. The other one was to rush to him.

"That sounds like..." Charlie straightened, too, looking over at me. "That sounds like Noah Worthington."

"It is Noah Worthington," I said, shoving my phone back in my pocket.

"Why is he here?" Charlie asked, standing up and looking at me as though I should have the answer to that.

We couldn't hear the men talking anymore. They had moved to another part of the house.

"I don't know," I said. And I really didn't. I might have known if I'd answered his messages earlier. But I'd been enjoying myself with Charlie and I hadn't wanted to be interrupted.

"Charlie," I said. "I have something to tell you."

He didn't seem to hear me.

"Charlie," I said again. "I need to tell you something."

Seeming to hear me now, he sat back down and met my gaze.

He must have seen something in my expression that told him just how important whatever it was I had to tell him was.

"I'm listening," he said.

I took a deep breath. A really deep breath and looking into Charlie's sparkling blue… troubled eyes.

It had been a good day.

One of the very best days I could remember having in a very long time.

I didn't want it to end.

But it was ending whether I wanted it to or not.

I started to put a hand on his arm, but then changed my mind.

"My name isn't Maggie," I said. "My name is Makenna Fleming."

He just stared blankly at me. "Why would you lie about that?" His expression was filled with suspicion and confusion and hurt.

I especially hated the suspicion in his eyes. I hated the way he was looking at me right now. Like he didn't know me. Or trust me or anything I said.

I turned away, looking into the flames, searching for answers where there weren't any.

"I don't have a good answer for that," I said.

"You're not my assistant then?"

"No."

He stood up again and walked to the window. I'm not sure how long he stood there, his back to me, but it seemed like forever.

I swallowed the panic that formed in the back of my throat.

I had no place to go if I left here.

But my grandfather was here. He would know what to do.

Grandpa Noah always knew what to do.

"I'm just gonna go upstairs to my room," I said.

I waited a moment, but Charlie didn't respond, so I simply slipped out of the living room and headed upstairs.

As I climbed the stairs, cheerful Christmas music spilled from a room off to my right.

Its cheerfulness seemed to mock the gut-wrenching sadness that filled me all the way through.

How was it that I had fallen for a guy in just one day?

I'd heard of such things, but I never thought it would happen to me.

I was much too logical.

Shaking my head, determined to get this figured out, I stepped into my guest room and closed the door behind me.

It wasn't supposed to happen like this.

It wasn't supposed to matter that I wasn't really his assistant.

I wasn't supposed to fall for him.

33

CHARLIE

I listened as Maggie... no... Makenna... left the living room and walked upstairs.

I should have said something to her. Anything.

But I was shell-shocked.

I had wished for this. I had wished for Maggie to not be my assistant. But I didn't expect it to happen. I didn't expect her to not only not be my assistant, but to be someone else entirely.

She was an imposter.

But why? Why was she pretending to be someone she wasn't?

I felt ripped in two.

Part of me, the cautious, logical part, wanted to kick her out of here on her heels. She wasn't honest. She was pretending to be someone else.

But another part of me wanted to hug her and sweep her off her feet. Kiss her right on the lips.

The thing that kept me immobilized was her name. Not Makenna. But *Fleming*.

I knew that name, but I couldn't get my brain to focus enough to pinpoint exactly where it was that I knew it from.

And I couldn't think with her sitting behind me. Now I couldn't think because she wasn't behind me.

I was a mess.

I went to stand in front of the fireplace, leaning an arm against the mantle.

As I stared into the flames, I tried to sort out exactly what had happened here.

The bottom line was there was nothing I could do about it right now. Not tonight.

Everything always looked better in the morning. Or so they said.

Father and Noah had gone back to Father's study and closed the door.

Whatever it was, I decided, it could wait until tomorrow.

I went upstairs, stopping for a moment in front of Makenna's door. It would have been so easy to knock on the door. To see her again. To let her explain.

She'd only been gone a few minutes and already I missed her.

The day we'd spent together had been one of the best days in my memory. It had been simple and easy.

But now I needed to leave her alone.

I needed to let things sort themselves out. And they would.

As much as it seemed like all was lost, I knew that things would happen the way they were supposed to.

It would all work out.

Right now I just needed to leave her alone.

She had made a brave admission.

And we both needed to rest.

We would regroup in the morning.

Sort it all out tomorrow.

I kept walking to my room. Stepped inside and closed the door behind me.

I tried to ignore the chill that swept over me.

She would be here tomorrow. Tomorrow I would find out who she really was and why she had impersonated my assistant.

There had to be a good reason.

34

MAKENNA

Wheels up.

Inside the cockpit was lit only by the lights of the plane's computers. Outside the little Gulfstream, was lit only by moonlight and starlight. Mostly moonlight and the landing lights.

This airplane, unlike the Phenom Charlie and I had flown in on this morning, was older. It was one of Grandpa's old standbys, sort of like the old pickup truck a guy kept around even though he had a Bentley in the garage.

Grandpa insisted that we take off tonight, leaving Whiskey Springs before the weather got unbearably bad.

It was dark, just a few snowflakes falling in the moonlight. But the roads were still clear, despite all the precautions, and the runway was dry.

Grandpa would know if it wasn't safe to fly.

He put safety above all else, especially when it came to his family.

One of his favorite sayings was that there were bold pilots and there are old pilots.

But there were no old bold pilots.

The plane left the ground gliding over the trees at the end of the short runway. We circled, then were flying due east while continuing to gain altitude.

Since Doc Alexander had given us a ride to the airport, we hadn't talked yet.

We didn't talk until we were in the air, then we spoke through our headsets.

"How is it you're here?" I asked, looking at him through the shadowy light of the headset.

"I had to drop Madison off in Denver."

That did not explain to me in the least how he came to be in Whiskey Springs. Whiskey Springs was not Denver.

"No. Here," I said. "Whiskey Springs."

"I could ask you the same thing," he said, not bothering to look in my direction since we couldn't see each other anyway.

"Betty," we both said at the same time.

"Betty said you had come up for a couple of days, but since the weather had turned bad, you'd be wanting a ride out."

I leaned back in my chair and ran my hands along my four-point harness.

What was Betty thinking? She hadn't asked me if I was ready to go.

Her timing was the worst.

Charlie and I had been having such a good day.

When Grandpa arrived, I knew I had to tell Charlie the truth. Unfortunately that had not gone well.

He hadn't even been able to face me, much less give me a chance to explain.

As far as he was concerned I was nothing but a liar and an imposter.

I couldn't blame him, of course. I would have thought the same.

"I figured you just caught a ride up to do some Christmas

shopping," he said with a shrug. "That's what Betty said, anyway.

I didn't have the energy to tell him the truth.

How could he understand it when I didn't?

And besides that, my heart ached too much. So much I could barely talk.

I stared out into the darkness of night and replayed my time with Charlie.

He'd turned out to be a lot different than my first impression of him.

He wasn't *grumpy*. He was *complex*.

Coming here to visit his parents after being away for ten years was a big deal. One that would have anyone disconcerted.

But Grandpa had swooped in, swept me away, and it was like I never even existed.

I'd told Charlie my real name, but he wouldn't associate my last name of Fleming with Noah Worthington. No one ever did unless they had reason.

Charlie would have no reason to make that association.

He'd made an impression on my heart.

One that would take some time to heal. I took a deep almost painful breath.

I just had to give it time.

35

CHARLIE

When I woke the next morning, I had that feeling, if only for a moment, that all was right with the world.

It was one of those feelings that if psychologists could bottle and sell, they could make a fortune.

But then I remembered that I had to sort things out with Maggie... no... Makenna.

The girl I'd spent the day with yesterday wasn't who she had claimed to be.

I just hoped the only thing she'd lied about was her name. I liked her the way she was.

Sweet. Charming. And a smile that couldn't be faked.

A beautiful megawatt charming smile that should be illegal.

She would have a good reason for impersonating my assistant.

As I stood in the shower, letting the hot water rush over my head, I contemplated some of those reasons.

Maybe it had started out as a mistake. A mistake that she had just gone with.

Maybe she needed a job. So she was showing me that she

could be a good assistant. Not that we had done anything even remotely related to work.

I absently picked up a bottle of shampoo and sudsed up my hair. Damned if the shampoo didn't smell like wildflowers and damned if it didn't remind me of Makenna.

The woman had gotten into my system and there was no getting her out.

It didn't really matter to me why she had lied about her name.

What difference did it make?

I still liked the girl. I loved the way her green eyes sparkled when she smiled at me. The way she always seemed to know the right thing to say.

I loved the way her hand felt in mine.

The way she looked like she belonged on a private jet. Like she belonged in that world. For all I knew, she did.

I regretted not saying anything to her last night when she'd confessed to who she really was.

Fortunately with the storm coming in, she couldn't go anywhere, so I could still talk to her.

Tell her I didn't care who she was.

I just wanted to spend time with her. To be with her.

By the time I stepped out of the shower and got dressed, sunlight was streaming through the bedroom window.

I walked to the window and looked out. There was no snow on the ground. No snow clouds in the sky.

It was like the snow had quite simply dissipated.

Grabbed my phone, I check my weather app. Then pulled up the local news.

Storm unexpectedly goes south.

Storm goes south.

The weather forecasters didn't normally get things THAT wrong.

So that meant that everything could go on as planned. The Christmas festivities could go on.

People could come and go as they pleased.

Speaking of, a pickup truck pulled into the driveway and parked. A man about my age got out, then went around and opened the passenger door for his girl.

Sliding my phone into the back pocket of my jeans, I left my room and headed down the hallway.

Momma was up. She'd made a big breakfast. Smelled like bacon and eggs.

I had to tell her about Makenna. Or maybe Makenna and I would keep that to ourselves, at least until we sorted it out.

As I started down the stairs in the quiet house, I did so with a feeling of dread.

36

MAKENNA

I spent the next day basically walking around in a daze. It was almost Christmas Eve. My most favorite day of the year.

Just one day to go.

And yet, my heart ached. I couldn't get Charlie out of my head.

I had just left. Just left. Without saying goodbye or anything.

It stung that he hadn't responded when I'd told him my real name. I felt like I had disappointed him.

And now I was here. I was here in Houston and he was there.

I liked Christmas Eve more than Christmas Day. On Christmas Day, everything was on its way back to normal. On Christmas Eve, there was still magic in the air. Anything was possible.

Since I still had shopping to do, I spent the day in the Galleria.

I bought presents for my siblings, my parents, and my grandparents.

Tomorrow evening was for my immediate family, then

Christmas day, the whole family would get together. Everyone. Aunts. Uncles. Cousins. But we didn't buy presents for each other. There were too many of us.

The Galleria was surprisingly not crowded for the day before Christmas Eve. Apparently I was one of the few who decided to wait until the last minute to doing my shopping.

As I was walking along the first floor near the skating rink, I passed a kiosk I hadn't noticed before.

It was odd that I hadn't noticed it because it had a rather magical look about it.

I stopped and just looked at all the snow globes on display. Dozens of them.

A young lady, dressed in a red gypsy costume with little bells jangling as she walked forward, a half smile on her face.

"These are beautiful," I said.

"Yes," the young lady said with a heavy accent. French, maybe. "They are magical."

"Magical." I stepped forward to take a closer look.

The young lady stepped aside. "You have sadness," she said.

I looked over at the girl. She wore heavy makeup, but she was quite beautiful and had a serene quality about her.

"Yes," I said. "Is it that obvious?"

"To me, yes."

I picked up one of the snow globes that had a Christmas tree in the middle of it. Turned it over and watched the falling snow.

I set the snow globe back down and started to walk away. I couldn't think of anyone in my family to buy one for. Maybe I'd come back by later.

"I show you special magical snow globe," the girl said.

Normally I wouldn't fall for sales tactics, but I was curious.

"Sit," the girl said indicating that I should sit on her stool.

I did as she asked.

Christmas music spilling from the mall's sound system changed into a happy wintery tune.

The gypsy girl bent down and opened a box, pulling out an empty glass snow globe.

"There's nothing inside it," I said as she set it in front of me.

Gypsy girl smiled. "It has everything inside it."

"What do you mean?" I leaned forward to take a closer look.

"You can pick it up," Gypsy girl said.

With a quick glance in her direction, I reached out and ran a hand along the snow globe. Unlike the others, it had nothing inside. No tree. No house. No little people.

"Is this a make your own kind of thing?" I asked.

"Something like that," she said with a wry smile.

I smiled back, feeling some of the sadness leave my eyes as I looked at Gypsy girl questioningly.

"Shake it," she said. "Then look inside very carefully."

"Okay," I said, picking up the snow globe and holding it in both hands. It was heavier than I expected. Definitely glass. Not plastic.

With a gentle shake, I set the snow inside the globe in motion.

I did as she said. I was nothing if not good at following directions.

As the snow swirled in the clear glass globe, an image began to form out of the murkiness.

The first thing that I saw clearly were... mountains. Mountains with snow clouds clustered around them.

Then the image zoomed in and I saw the little Main Street of Whiskey Springs.

This wasn't a regular snow globe. This was some kind of image. Like looking through a window into another world.

As I looked more closely, the image continued to clear and focus in.

And then it went into motion. Twinkling Christmas lights.

I saw people walking along the sidewalks.

I was fascinated. Unable to look away.

As the seconds ticked past, the images became even more clear.

Then I saw us.

I saw me and Charlie walking hand in hand in the beautiful falling snow.

I gasped and put my nose against the glass so I could see better. If I could have, I would have stepped through the glass into the snow globe.

It was so real, I could almost hear the music as it flowed through the speakers.

The Charlie and I in the snow globe stopped and faced each other, holding both hands. We smiled at each other.

Then he kissed me.

I blinked and jerked back.

How the—

I glanced over at Gypsy girl, but she was busy dusting the other regular snow globes with a duster.

I looked back at the snow globe in my hands but it was empty now. Just snow and water or whatever fluid was inside the glass.

I shook it. But the image didn't reappear.

"Where did it go?" I asked.

Gypsy girl met my gaze, that same little grin on her lips.

"Did you see something?"

"I saw…" I took a deep breath. "What does it mean?"

"That snow globe has a name," she said. "It's called the Magic of Christmas. It shows us what our heart knows can be true."

I shook it again. "How?"

"It's magic," she said. "They tell me that whatever image you saw is only good until Midnight Christmas Eve, then it just become a memory of what could have been."

A memory...

Christmas Eve.

My hands trembling, I carefully set the snow globe back on the shelf, then stood up.

My legs felt a little wobbly.

"How much?" I asked, wondering how much I needed to pay her.

She waved me off.

"Just go," she said. "Do not worry."

Dashing past other shoppers, I strode toward the escalator.

As I rode up, I pulled my phone out of my pocket.

"Grandpa," I said. "I need your help."

37

CHARLIE

The town was abuzz with festivities.

Last night had been the Festival of Trees and tonight was the North Pole Express—mostly for children.

The North Pole Express was a little narrow-gauge train that traveled around the outside of town, ending up at the town's little convention center where the children could sit on Santa's lap and tell him what they really wanted for Christmas.

It seemed a bit late in the season for that, to me at least. How was Santa supposed to pull miracles out of his hat the day before Christmas Eve? But that's how they did it.

Couples also rode the train, using it as a romantic ride like a hay ride or a carriage ride.

Having neither children nor anyone to ride the train with, I merely walked along downtown.

Since no one really knew me, I was left alone with my own thoughts.

Those thoughts consisted almost completely of Makenna Fleming.

I knew exactly who she was now.

She was Noah Worthington's granddaughter.

Sister to Daniel Fleming. That was, in fact, how I had figured it out.

Daniel Fleming and his fiancé Jenna had stopped by my parents' house to deliver some cookies.

That's when it had all fit together for me.

Daniel Fleming, a pilot, was moving to Whiskey Springs and was going to be the pilot working out of the Whiskey Springs airport.

I didn't know why Makenna had pretended to be my assistant or why she had come to Whiskey Springs with me, but I knew it wasn't because she needed the work.

I soon learned that Makenna was a venture capitalist, an expert, in fact, in green energy. She was an independent contractor.

An entrepreneur like her grandfather, it seems.

So I still didn't have an explanation for how the whole thing happened, but whatever her reason, it wasn't for any kind of monetary gain.

Maybe she had just been swept away in the moment. It could happen. But then I had acted like an ass. So she had left.

Each shop I passed played a different Christmas song that blended in the songs piped over the outside speakers.

It would be dark soon and already the streets were lit up with twinkling lights.

I stopped in front of one of the General Stores to admire the window display.

It was filled with a little town that looked a lot like Whiskey Springs.

A little miniature train ran through it, over a hill, through a little tunnel and back again.

It was magical.

I could almost see it coming to life.

It didn't take a lot of imagination to see the little wooden figures moving about, going about their business just as they were doing in real life.

I shook my head. I was being fanciful.

With my heart aching, I wasn't thinking clearly.

I'd been torturing myself like crazy. Now that I knew who Makenna was, I could find her.

That was not a problem.

The problem was whether or not she wanted to see me.

I'd bungled that up badly.

I was going to find a way to fix it.

I just didn't know what that was yet.

At the moment, I was trying to figure out how to get myself out of Whiskey Springs. Noah Worthington had flown me up here, only to leave me stranded.

As far as I could tell, I hadn't done anything wrong, not really... not professionally at least... but he hadn't sent anyone to pick me up.

So I had to find my own way out of here.

That meant it would be after Christmas before I could get back to Houston.

I opened the door and went into the General Store. Maybe I could find gifts for my parents.

Since I was here, I might as well make the most of it.

38

MAKENNA

Christmas Eve

The sleek Phenom locked into place for a landing at the Whiskey Springs airport.

Grandpa himself was the pilot.

Far below, the late-day sunshine glinted off the blue spruce trees and the little patches of snow beneath them.

The snow storm had gone south. Very unusual for the forecasters to get it so wrong. No one faulted them for it. It was, after all, the weather. The weather could quite simply change without warning.

My heart started beating a little faster at the clunk of the wheels going down.

I was basing all this—being here—on the image I saw in a magical snow globe.

But I knew what I saw.

I saw myself in Whiskey Springs. With Charlie.

I had no doubt about that.

It had been magical.

I had no doubt about what I had seen.

I had every doubt about why and how it had happened.

But I'd heard of stranger things.

Grandpa went in for a landing, the wheels touching down smoothly on the tarmac.

It was a short runway, but he navigated it smoothly.

Grandpa was nearly seventy years old, but didn't look a day over fifty. He was a handsome clean-cut man who carried himself with the confidence his success had earned him. And he was kind. And fair. There was no one else like Noah Worthington.

"Do you want me to wait for you?" he asked.

He'd asked me that before, but I had the same answer I'd had before.

"No," I said with a little smile. "I'm trusting the process."

I had to. Having come this far, I had to go all in.

"That's all you can do," he said. "It's what you should do."

"I'm sorry I won't be home for Christmas," I said.

"You'll be there next year," he said. "And my gut says you won't be alone."

I smiled, owning the nervous jitters in my stomach.

"Is that how it was with you and Grandma?" I asked.

Grandpa began going through the post landing checklist.

The construction site was deserted, so there was no reason to worry about parking the plane too close. Not today.

"It's hard to describe what Grandma and I had from the very beginning. I guess you could just call it love at first sight. Unfortunately I almost let my family destroy it. I don't recommend that. In fact, I can't let it happen to you."

We unbuckled our harnesses and removed our headsets.

"I insist that you follow your heart."

"Thanks, Grandpa." I leaned over and gave him a hug.

"Looks like your car is here," he said.

I looked up to see a white sedan making its way toward us.

We disembarked from the plane and Grandpa unloaded my two suitcases.

Five minutes later, I was on my way toward Whiskey Springs. Alone this time.

And Grandpa was taking the plane back to Houston.

I was all in now.

The drunken butterflies fluttered in my stomach making me feel rather queasy as we made our way down the road toward Main Street.

It was already dusk, already dark enough that our way was lit almost completely by the car's headlights.

Sitting in the backseat, I stared out the window. There was just enough dusky light for me to see two elk standing on the side of the road, their ears twitching as they watched us pass.

I smiled to myself as I imagined the elk actually being reindeer getting ready for their big night flying around the world dropping off magical presents everywhere.

The only present I wanted was to be with Charlie.

I bit my lip as I fretted. What if he wasn't here? What if he didn't want to see me?

Then I remembered what I had seen in the snow globe and it fortified my decision to be here.

"Where am I taking you, Miss?" the driver asked.

I truly had not gotten that far.

"The saloon," I said, not knowing where else to land. I couldn't just walk up to Charlie's parents' front door with my two suitcases. I was not that bold.

I didn't have a room at the saloon. I had come here without a reservation of any kind. And my brother was in Houston. So the only person here I knew was Charlie.

Blind faith. Or something like that.

The driver pulled up outside the saloon and, after opening

my door and helping me out, took my luggage from the trunk and stood it on the sidewalk.

Without asking, he opened the door to the saloon and rolled my luggage inside.

There were only three people sitting at the tables. Apparently the water leak wasn't fixed yet.

The bartender recognized me. Good memory, especially since I hadn't even spoken to him when I'd been here before.

"I know I don't have a reservation," I said. "Can I just leave my luggage here for a little while?"

"Of course," he said. "I'll take care of it."

So far everything was falling into place.

With nothing left to do, except go and find Charlie, I pulled my woolen coat closer before stepping back outside onto the sidewalk.

I started walking aimlessly down the sidewalk, heading east. My hands in my pockets. The cold wind swept at my hair and I felt a bit silly.

Although I could have gotten it, I didn't have Charlie's phone number. I'd decided to just show up out of the blue.

It was Christmas Eve and that was what I had seen in the magical snow globe.

If I was going to find Charlie, I had to do it today. Before the magic expired.

They tell me that whatever image you saw is only good until Midnight Christmas Eve, then it just become a memory of what could have been.

A memory...

I stopped and watched a couple dart into one of the stores, getting out of the cold.

I should march right up to the Alexander's house. It wasn't like I had a lot of time to waste.

I stopped at the General Store to admire the window display. There was a little miniature train running around over little mountains through a little town. All it needed was a little snow and it would have looked like its own magical snow globe scene.

But not like *my* magical snow globe scene.

As I stood there watching the little train run round and round, the door to the General Store opened, letting the strains of a Christmas carol spill out and mingle with the other song spilling out of the speakers on the sidewalk.

The hair on the back of my neck tingled.

I turned slowly and looked over at the man who had just stepped outside.

Charlie.

He blinked as he looked at me.

"Makenna?" he asked. My name sounded strange on his lips. I'd only heard him call me Maggie.

"Charlie." I took a step forward, then stopped.

"How—"

I just shrugged with a little smile.

"You're really here."

"I'm really here."

He closed the distance between us, grabbed me around the waist, and twirled me around in a circle.

A song about how wonderful this time of year was spilled over the speakers. I agreed completely.

Everything was beautiful.

Then Charlie set me on my feet and, holding both my hands, leaned forward and kissed me.

Just like in the magical snow globe.

I was right where I was supposed to be on this magical Christmas Eve.

39

CHARLIE

It was Christmas Eve and I had two more gifts to buy.

My sister, Bella, had come home for Christmas.

My mother was ecstatic that she had both of her children home for Christmas. I'd never seen her so happy.

Bella had come with a boyfriend in tow, so we had a full house.

I bought gift cards. I know it was a copout, but I did it anyway. At least they could get something they wanted. I could have sent ecards, but I preferred to give the plastic kind that I could wrap up and put under the tree.

The brightly colored lights twinkled up and down Main Street as I stepped outside onto the sidewalk. Two Christmas songs blended seamlessly into one. It seemed like it would be discordant, but it wasn't. It was actually rather pleasing.

A few light snowflakes were falling. Maybe it was going to snow after all. It was possible the weather guys had missed the timing, not the forecast.

Snowfall on Christmas Eve was beautiful and, like

everything else, made me think of Makenna. How she'd turned her face up to the snow and turned around in a circle.

A movement off to my left caught my attention. Maybe it wasn't a movement so much as it was a feeling.

I stopped and slowly turned.

A woman stood there, staring at the window display much as I had yesterday.

If I hadn't known better…

I recognized her black woolen coat. I recognized the hair falling loosely around her shoulders.

And when she turned, I recognized her.

It was a miracle.

It was Makenna.

"Makenna?"

When she smiled, any residual doubt I had that it was her dissipated.

But how?

How didn't matter so much as I picked her up and twirled her in a circle.

Not wanting to have another regret, I pressed my lips lightly against hers.

"Makenna," I said, leaning back and sweeping a lock of hair off her face.

Keeping my hands on hers, looking into her eyes, I saw a single tear falling slowly from the corner of her eye, making its way down her cheek.

"Oh, sweetheart," I said, kissing the tear away. "You're here and that's all that matters."

She nodded and gazed into my eyes.

"Where's your luggage?" I asked.

"The saloon."

"Let's get it and go home."

She nodded again, but her bottom lip was trembling.

"Are you okay?"

"I'm so happy," she said, her voice barely audible.

I reached into my pocket and pulled out my white handkerchief.

My father had been right after all.

Always have a handkerchief on hand in case a lady needs it.

And finally, after all these years, I found the lady who needed it.

And who would have thought?

She needed it because she was happy.

This was truly a magical Christmas.

Keep Reading for a preview of
SECOND CHANCE KISSES...

PREVIEW SECOND CHANCE KISSES
MADISON WORTHINGTON

This was not happening.

Not in a hundred years.

I stared at the schedule on the computer screen in front me. The caller on the other end of the phone line forgotten.

The least of my problems.

I forgot to breathe. Or maybe I just couldn't get any air.

How many Kade Johnsons were there?

How many Kade Samuel Johnsons?

How many Kade Samuel Johnsons who were pilots?

"Hello?"

Right. I was scheduling a flight for Markus Peters. One of Skye Travel's best customers.

Shit.

"I'm so sorry Mr. Peters. There was a glitch in the phone line." There was actually a glitch in my brain.

It had been eight years since I'd seen Kade Johnson.

Eight years.

And not a day in those eight years had passed that I hadn't had at least a fleeting thought of Kade Johnson in one way or another.

I put Mr. Peters on speaker and keyed in his information. He now had a flight to Florida with his family scheduled for Friday.

With Kade Johnson in the pilot's seat.

My little brother, Quinn, was going to hear about this. Had Quinn lost his mind?

"Thank you, Mr. Peters, for flying Skye Travels. We'll see you Friday."

I clicked off the phone and looked toward the conference room.

Fortunately for Quinn, he was tied up in a meeting for the next... I glanced at my watch... hour or so.

And by then, I'd be heading out.

It was only my first day on the job—sort of, but I'd been doing this work on and off, since I was a senior in high school.

A questionable perk of being the boss's daughter.

My father, Noah Worthington, believed his children should work like everyone else.

He didn't want us growing up soft, living off his money. And all five of his children had careers.

The only questionable one, though, was my little brother Quinn.

He'd gotten his business degree, then somehow slid right into the company as vice-president.

He claimed to be following in our father's footsteps, but I seemed to be the only one who noticed that Quinn had never flown an airplane.

Our father, however, was a well-known and respected pilot and had formed his company, Skye Travels, based on that reputation.

I could see the tarmac from here. Close enough that the office carried the comforting scent of jet fuel. But right now even that wasn't enough to calm my nerves.

I had to get through the next hour. Then I could figure out what to do about this Kade Johnson thing.

I straightened up what was going to be my workspace for the next three months and checked my phone messages.

I had one text from my best friend Emily.

EMILY: *Are you off yet?*

ME: *Not yet. One hour left.*

EMILY: *Drinks at the Skyhouse?*

She completely read my mind. I'd only been back in town a few days and hadn't seen my best friend yet.

ME: *OMG. Yes.*

EMILY: *See you there.*

My fingers hovered over the keys. But I set my phone down. I wasn't ready to tell her about Kade. I was still processing it myself and I didn't need Emily's opinion tossed into my brain just yet.

Quinn stuck his head out of the conference room across the hall.

"Madison? Would you make some copies for us?"

"Of course." I put a big fake smile on my face for the benefit of the two men who were meeting with Quinn as I took the envelope from him.

The men were from a big marketing firm and Quinn was meeting them to set up a contract. I had to give Quinn credit. He was good at schmoozing.

But seriously. Quinn was taking advantage of me.

I should have a nameplate made for the receptionist desk.

Dr. Madison Worthington.

I squared my shoulders. I'd done it to myself. I was the one who'd volunteered to help out until he could hire someone for the summer. And then I'd be the one to train the new person.

The receptionist they'd had for years had retired last week. I had trained her myself during the summer before I left for graduate school. I seriously think she waited until she knew I was coming in for the summer before she announced it.

I didn't blame her. This way I was the one doing the training.

My father's work ethic was firmly cemented in my psyche.

I didn't begrudge it. That work ethic was what had gotten me through undergrad in three years. Then graduate school.

After getting my license to practice psychology, I'd done some teaching at Houston Community College and discovered that I liked it. Okay. Loved it.

At first, I couldn't believe they were paying me to do something that was so much fun.

It hadn't taken me long to land a full-time teaching job.

In Denver.

I had three months before I had to show up for new faculty orientation.

Since I already had my apartment secured, I had some time on my hands.

The copy room was at the other end of the office suite. Past the elevator.

Just as I stepped past the elevator, it dinged.

Skye Travels was known for not only its efficiency, but also its Houston hospitality.

I turned, holding the brown envelope Quinn had handed me against my chest and prepared to greet whoever stepped off the elevator.

But also, Quinn was waiting.

I took a step backwards.

The elevator doors opened.

And I froze.

Kade Samuel Johnson stepped off the elevator.

I was having that breathing problem again.

Maybe I should see a doctor about that.

But I already knew it was full-fledged anxiety.

And I knew how to treat it. I was a psychologist after all.

Take a deep breath.

Kade stepped out of the elevator. Stopped and looked right at me.

It was almost like he'd known I was standing there.

He wouldn't have known, of course.

Couldn't have known.

He looked at me blankly.

He didn't even recognize me.

We'd been together for three years and he didn't even recognize me.

I clamped down every thought that came to my head.

Kade worked here now.

My stupid, inconsiderate, clueless brother had hired him.

So I just turned around.

I turned around and continued to the copy room.

I wasn't about to let Kade Johnson know that I'd thought about him every day when he couldn't even have the decency to recognize me.

Sure. It had been eight years.

Sure. Instead of actually breaking up, we'd drifted apart.

But still.

I stepped into the copy room and opened the envelope.

My hands were shaking too much for me to do the simple task of pulling the papers out of the envelope and my eyes wouldn't focus.

Damn it.

This was not going to get the best of me.

I yelped as the envelope sliced across my right index finger giving me a paper cut.

I dropped the envelope onto the copier and stuck my bleeding finger in my mouth.

When I'd gotten up this morning, I'd had no idea that this would be the day I'd see Kade Johnson again.

And all the psychological training in the world was useless.

KADE JOHNSON

I recognized Madison immediately, of course.

But I swear my body knew she was there before I did.

As soon as the elevator dinged and the door opened, it knew.

I'd always liked the scent of jet fuel, but it had never been a turn on.

Not like that.

It was definitely Madison.

By the time my brain caught up, she'd turned around and walked away.

My first instinct was to follow her. And I even took two steps forward before my logical brain reminded me that my instinct was eight years out of date.

She'd always been pretty. With a quick smile.

But the Madison who'd just walked away from me was not pretty. She was drop dead gorgeous.

Long, brunette mermaid hair. That perfect heart-shaped face. Lips that naturally turned up at the corners.

And a tight black skirt that did everything to remind me what I knew about that body beneath it.

She was wearing a white button-down shirt tucked into that skirt, revealing her narrow waist.

I bet I could still wrap my hands around that waist.

But I worked here now. And she was the boss's daughter.

I had to keep it together.

And keep it in my pants.

I needed a minute before I walked down to reception to meet up with Quinn.

The last thing I needed was to walk into my new office with a hard-on.

I'd only met Quinn Worthington once and during the interview calls, neither one of us had mentioned my previous relationship with his sister. It was possible he didn't even remember me from back then.

Not likely. But certainly possible.

He was younger than I was. Five years? Maybe more.

And when I'd been with Madison, Quinn had been away at a boarding school or some such to prep him for college.

It occurred to me then that Quinn might have hired me without telling Madison.

And if Madison worked here...

I thought she'd be far away from here by now.

I'd seen enough social media updates—not stalking—to know that she'd finished her degree in psychology.

She'd finished it just like she'd set out to do.

Madison completed everything she set out to do. It was one of the many things I admired about her.

Unfortunately, though, it had been the end of our relationship.

We'd decided not to do the whole long distance thing.

I don't know what she'd been thinking, but I always sort of thought we were on a break.

I'd dated, of course. It had been eight years after all and a man had needs.

But I'd never let myself get serious with anyone.

Was it because of Madison?

Not that I would ever admit it.

I turned left and went toward what looked like a lobby. All my interviews and discussions had been via FaceTime. My reputation was good enough to get me a job anywhere in the industry.

But life happened and I needed to be closer to home.

There was no one at the receptionist's desk. Quinn was in

the glass-walled conference room on the other end of the lobby with two men.

I took a seat on one of the little sofas in the spacious lobby. This whole side of the office had floor to ceiling windows overlooking the tarmac.

I had an involuntary little sense of excitement. This third floor office space was perfect.

I should have known Noah Worthington would do it right. The man had gone from being a commercial pilot—like me—to owning a fleet of small jets. He had started out in Dallas/Fort Worth, but for some unknown reason, he'd moved his main office to Houston.

Rumors suggested it had something to do with his wife Savannah. And apparently they were living in Houston now.

The receptionist must have already left for the day. Not a problem. I didn't have anything else I had to do today.

I stretched out my legs and pulled out my iPad. Scrolled idly through my emails.

But. Damn it. I couldn't concentrate.

Madison was somewhere in this office. I know she recognized me, but she'd turned walked away.

At the sound of feminine heels coming toward me from the elevator area, I looked up.

And watched as Madison walked straight toward me.

I stood up. Bad idea.

All the blood had rushed to my center.

Then she smiled and I nearly came undone.

Keep Reading SECOND CHANCE KISSES...

Kathryn Kaleigh is the author of over seventy novels, over one hundred short stories, and many collections.

kathrynkaleigh.com